The Truth About
Rats
(and Dogs)

to Ashley

Jacqueline Pearce

Rats rule!

Jacqueline Pearce

ORCA BOOK PUBLISHERS

Library and Archives Canada Cataloguing in Publication

Pearce, Jacqueline, 1962-

The truth about rats (and dogs) / Jacqueline Pearce.

ISBN 1-55143-473-3

I. Title.

PS8581.E26T78 2006   jC813'.6   C2006-903255-6

First published in the United States, 2006
Library of Congress Control Number: 2006928466

Summary: Conner's family has a no-pets rule, but Oscar the rat needs a home.

Orca Book Publishers gratefully acknowledges the support for its publishing programs provided by the following agencies: the Government of Canada through the Book Publishing Industry Development Program and the Canada Council for the Arts, and the Province of British Columbia through the BC Arts Council and the Book Publishing Tax Credit.

Cover design and typesetting by Doug McCaffry
Cover illustration by Susan Reilly

Orca Book Publishers
Box 5626, Stn. B
Victoria, BC Canada
v8R 6s4

Orca Book Publishers
PO Box 468
Custer, WA USA
98240-0468

www.orcabook.com

Printed and bound in Canada
09 08 07 06 • 4 3 2 1

For all kids who love animals

Acknowledgments

I would like to thank my friends Yee Tse and Annette Fung for sharing with me their families' experiences of Chinese New Year, and Mr. and Mrs. Tse for treating me to lunch and answering my many questions. Thank you to Gord Hobbis and Jordan Masse of Cap's Bicycle Shop in New Westminster/Sapperton for sharing their expertise on BMX bikes and stunts; Rebecca Chen and Olga Stancovick for their help with piano info; Randy Celinski of AAA Wildlife for his insights on wild rats and methods for dealing with them; my mom, Rochelle Pearce (former nurse and recent patient), for answering medical questions; the BC SPCA Animal Learning Centre for lending me Oscar; Alley Allen for showing me the small-animal room at the BC SPCA's Vancouver shelter; and all the other friends (especially the Nelson School playground moms) who answered my various queries and offered encouragement and support.

Contents

Torture

My fingers stumbled along the keys. Every day I started piano practice with scales. Every Saturday I started piano lessons with scales. The plunk of the keys was beginning to feel like Chinese water torture, each note a painful drip. Is that a real thing? Chinese water torture, I mean. Or is it one of those weird ideas Western people have about Chinese people? I'll have to ask my dad.

C D E F G A B C.

Chinese piano torture is definitely real. When you are half Chinese, people seem to expect the Chinese half to make you good at piano or violin or math. It doesn't help when your older sister is good at everything.

"Conner, are you paying attention?"

Miss Remple, my piano teacher, stood behind my right shoulder, looming over me like a police interrogator getting ready to squeeze a confession out of her prisoner. Except her voice was a little too high-pitched for the mean cop role, and she sounded more exasperated than threatening.

"Watch your fingering," she warned.

I tried to focus more carefully on what my fingers were doing to the piano keys, and I felt Miss Remple relax slightly behind me. At the end of the scale the notes died away, and Miss Remple took a sip of coffee from the mug she always held throughout the lesson. For a second, the sound of her swallowing was the only noise in the room. I repressed a shiver. I hated that sound. She obviously had no idea how unnerving it was. How was anyone supposed to concentrate with that gurgly swallowing sound right behind their ear? Every time I heard her swallow, it was as if that sound in her throat was saying, *Your playing stinks!*

"Now, let's hear how you're doing with the minuet," Miss Remple said.

The minuet. My parents were so thrilled that I was learning a Mozart minuet. I guess they thought it meant I was actually progressing. My sister, Jenna, said it was an easy piece to play, but I didn't seem to be able to get it right.

I fumbled with the pages of the music book on the ledge above the piano keys, wishing I could stop feeling nervous. It was so stupid. I played for Miss Remple every weekend. Why didn't it get any easier?

"There you go." Miss Remple reached across and stuck a finger on the page before I could flip past the minuet.

Her sleeve brushed my shoulder, and the smell of perfume and coffee breath made me queasy. I turned aside to sneak a breath of fresher air. Was the room getting smaller? The walls seemed closer, like I really was locked inside a tiny windowless interrogation room.

Okay, stop fooling around. Just get it over with. I took a few extra seconds finding the first notes on the page and settling my hands over the keys. Miss Remple sighed and took another sip of coffee. Quickly, I began to play, figuring I could at least drown out the gurgling swallow.

"That wasn't too bad," Miss Remple said as I finished the piece. I could tell she was trying to sound encouraging because that was how piano teachers were supposed to sound or all their students would just give up.

"You've pretty much got the notes down," she continued.

Finally, I thought. I'd only practiced the thing every day for two weeks.

"Now you need to work on expression," she added.

I groaned inwardly.

Expression? I didn't even *like* Mozart. I didn't even like classical music. How was I supposed to put *expression* into it when I didn't even like piano? But then, nobody cared how I felt about things anyway.

Finally the lesson ended and I was released. Outside, I took in a deep breath of cool January air and freedom, pulled my bike helmet on and jumped on my bike. I cranked hard on the pedals, trying to get as much distance as possible, as quickly as possible, between me and piano lessons. After picking up some speed, I glided for a while, scoping the street for a clear driveway and a high curb. There, up ahead. The spot where the curb sloped down to the driveway entrance made a perfect ramp. I veered into the driveway, rode up the curb and launched into the air.

Sweet!

I was airborne for only a few seconds, but for those seconds I was free. It was so good to be out of that stuffy piano room. For the rest of the day I could do whatever I wanted. Probably after lunch I'd meet my friend Jake and we'd work on some bike tricks. There was a flatland BMX competition coming up next month that we thought we might enter. Or maybe we'd try our bikes on the quarter pipe at the new skateboard park.

It was only a few blocks from Miss Remple's house to mine and not long before I was pulling into our driveway. My plan was to park my bike in the backyard and head inside for a quick lunch. I braked at the back gate. As I pushed it open, I heard a scream.

Invader

The scream—well, maybe it was more of a screech—was followed by an angry voice that sounded like my mom's. Had she been the one screaming? I had a vision of a burglar sneaking into the back of the house and attacking her. The vision quickly shifted to an image of my mother attacking the burglar, as I heard another yell, followed by a crash. Not sure what to expect, I dropped my bike and rushed through the gate into the backyard.

I rounded the corner of the house just in time to see Mom smash a broom down on the lid of the garbage can that sat beside the back steps. There was no sign of a burglar.

"Mom, are you okay?"

Her short dark-blond hair, which was normally very neat and stylish, was a little wild, and there was a grim expression on her face, but otherwise she didn't look like she'd been attacked.

"Stay back!" she warned me, and the look on her face made me take a step backward.

"Why? What's going on?" I asked, glancing quickly around the yard. Maybe there really was a burglar.

Mom's eyes darted back to the garbage can. She swung the broom and thumped the side of the can. What *was* she doing? My mind jumped to visions of robotic garbage cans trying to climb the stairs to the house.

"Is it gone?" Mom asked.

"Is what gone?" I still had no idea what was wrong.

"The rat!" she screeched, her voice rising at least one octave higher than usual (octaves are one thing I *did* learn about at piano lessons).

I looked around the garbage can and under the stairs, half expecting to see a large brown rat with long yellow teeth and beady evil eyes crouching and glaring at me. But there was nothing there.

"I don't see anything," I said. "You must have scared it away."

"Are you sure?" Mom asked. Then she blocked me with the broom. "Don't get too close," she warned again. "Rats carry disease, and they can bite."

I rolled my eyes. Anything that threatened to bring dirt or germs anywhere near my mom or her kitchen was definitely risking its life, and judging by how fast she had wielded that broom, it didn't have much chance of getting near me, either. Still, I didn't feel inclined to take any chances, so I kept my distance.

"Are you sure it was a rat," I asked, "and not the neighbor's cat?"

"Of course I'm sure," Mom snapped, but she lowered the broom.

"Look," she said, pointing to the garbage can lid.

Despite the battering taken by the garbage can, two small black droppings remained on the green plastic lid. They definitely hadn't been left by the neighbor's cat.

"Don't touch it!" Mom yelled as I took a step closer.

The panic in her voice startled me and made me jump back.

"I wasn't going to touch it!" *Geesh! What did she think I was? An idiot?*

"Sorry," she said with a grimace. "I don't like the idea of having a rat around, spreading germs so close to the house…And what if there's more than one?"

I suppressed a shudder as I imagined a dark wave of rats sweeping over our garbage can and up the stairs to the house. I'd seen a picture like that in a book about the Middle Ages and the Plague.

"Come on," Mom said, starting up the stairs. "Let's go in for lunch. There's nothing else we can do right now. I'll call your dad and ask him to pick up a rat trap on his way home."

"I'll be right there," I called after her. "I just have to bring in my bike."

I went back to the gate and wheeled my bike into the yard. Were rats really that bad? I was sure Dad didn't know any more about catching rats than Mom did. An idea flared in my head. There were dogs that were bred to catch rats, weren't there?

I hadn't worked on my parents about getting a dog for almost a year now. *No pets!* they always said, even though I'd wanted a dog more than anything ever since I was little. I'd even promised to practice the piano harder if they'd let me get a dog, but they wouldn't go for it. The rat angle was new, though. Maybe it was worth a try.

I leaned my bike against the stairs and ran up the steps, taking them two at a time. What was the name of that rat-catching dog? I was sure I'd read about it in my dog book.

"Take your shoes off," Mom said as I came through the back door, even though I was already doing just that.

I shucked off my runners without undoing the laces and left them on the mat by the door, then hung up my jacket on the wall hook.

"Make sure you wash your hands really well before you touch anything," Mom added predictably.

She stood at the counter with her back to me, so she couldn't see the face I made. Even if there hadn't been a rat infesting the yard with germs, she would still have reminded me to wash my hands. She's never figured out that I always wash without her asking, and I always take my shoes off when I come inside. She'll probably phone and remind me when I'm old and living on my own.

I caught myself before saying anything that might sound rude, remembering that, if anything, I should be trying to butter her up.

"Okay, Mom," I said cheerfully as I headed down the hall to the washroom.

The Right Dog

After I'd washed my hands, I ducked into my room and pulled *The Complete Guide to Dogs* off the bookshelf over my desk. The large heavy hardcover felt solid and satisfying in my hands. I opened it at random. The chapter heading was Working Dogs. There was a photograph of a large dog, mostly black, with a white chest and some brown on its legs and face. The caption beside the dog was "Bernese mountain dog." It looked like a nice dog, but it was large, and I was sure the rat-catching dog I'd read about had been small enough to go down holes after its prey. I flipped through the pages, looking for smaller dogs. I stopped at dachshund in the Hounds section. That one looked promising.

"Dachs" is badger in German, and this dog was used for flushing badgers out of their setts.

I assumed that setts meant burrows, but it wasn't the right dog either. I didn't really like the look of the dachshund anyway. Too much like a giant wiener. I flipped through the rest of the Hounds section and moved on to the Gun Dogs. There sure seemed to be a lot of dogs bred to help with hunting. But I guessed hunting was what people depended on for survival in the old days. I paused at the Labrador retriever, which was one of my favorite dogs.

A chocolate Lab, that's what I really wanted. I imagined myself running across the field at my school, a big brown dog running beside me. I'd throw a stick or a ball and the dog would run to get it.

"Conner, are you coming for lunch?" Mom's voice cut through my daydream.

"In a minute!" I called back.

I flipped through the book more quickly until I hit Terriers.

Originally bred to hunt rats and other vermin, they were developed to chase out quarry that had gone to ground, often by actually digging it out of burrows.

That sounded right. But what kind of terrier? I read further.

There was the Airedale terrier, the fox terrier, the bull terrier. When I got to the Jack Russell terrier, I stopped. That was it. That was the dog I'd been thinking of.

I read on, learning a lot about Jack Russells before I came to anything about rats. What I found out was pretty gross.

Jack Russells were often used in the sport of rat killing, which was popular in England in the early part of the twentieth century. The sport involved penning a large number of rats, then throwing in a dog to see how many rats the dog could kill and how quickly he could do it.

People sure used to have weird ideas of entertainment. But the dog definitely sounded up to the task of ridding our backyard of one rat (at least I hoped there was just one).

I brought the book out to the kitchen.

"Listen to this, Mom." I read out the part about the rats.

"Please, Conner, not while we're eating lunch," Mom complained as she ladled steaming noodle soup into a bowl over the stovetop. There was a sandwich waiting at my place at the table.

I slid into a chair, my eyes still on the book as Mom set the bowl of soup in front of me.

"It says here that Jack Russells are very intelligent and attentive to their owners," I continued. "They can be tough, determined, devoted, loyal." I skipped the part about them being feisty and sometimes hard to manage.

Mom sighed.

"Conner, we've been through this before. We are not going to get a dog—or any other pet, for that matter."

"But a dog like the Jack Russell could keep the rats away."

"It's just one rat," Mom said sternly. "We'll get a trap, and that will be that. Pets have germs, and you know how I feel about germs or pet hairs in my kitchen."

Disappointment and frustration expanded like a balloon in my chest. What had I been expecting, anyway? I'd tried all the arguments before. Why would this time be any different? Even if Mom didn't run a catering business out of her kitchen, she'd still be a clean freak. But I couldn't help trying one more time.

"Jack Russells have short hair," I pointed out. "They don't shed much, and I could always . . ." My voice trailed off as Mom turned away, shaking her head.

I glared at my soup in frustration. She wasn't even listening to me.

I heard Mom sigh.

"Conner," she began, her voice softer as she turned to face me again. I could tell she wanted me to understand her reasons and not be upset, but I didn't look up. Before she could say any more, the front door opened and Jenna's voice came from the front hall. She had one of her friends with her.

Mom turned to greet them—a little too eagerly, I thought.

"No one listens to me in this house," I grumbled into my soup. At least I could complain at the animal club meeting next week. Erika and the others would understand.

"Oh, and Conner," Mom said, turning back to me and lowering her voice, "don't say anything about the rat to anyone—especially your grandmother."

School

"Green light for the shelter," a girl's voice announced close behind me as the grade sixes filed into the classroom on Monday morning. I glanced back as Erika Leveson and Mercedes Sharma squeezed past me. Their eyes met mine, and we exchanged grins. *Green light* meant the arrangements had been made for the club to visit the animal shelter for our Wednesday meeting.

Perfect. Doing something with animals would be way better than just talking about them. True, we did spend time with Daisy, the guinea pig in Mrs. Ferguson's class, but she was already well looked after by twenty-five grade two kids.

Since we'd formed the animal club back in November, we'd met every Wednesday after school. Mrs. Ferguson had volunteered to be our sponsor because she liked animals and thought kids could learn from them. The grade twos took turns feeding and taking care of Daisy every day, but on Wednesdays the animal club members helped change the bedding and clip Daisy's toenails if they needed it. We'd also made Daisy a larger habitat out of a big box with places for her to explore and hide. It was more interesting for her than her small cage.

Besides helping with Daisy, the club also talked about animal issues and worked on projects. In December we'd had a big *Remember the Animals* campaign and collected old blankets, towels, animal toys and stuff that we donated to the local animal shelter. We'd also invited guest speakers to come and talk to us. Our first guest speaker had been Erika's mom, who told us about her job as a vet. She'd also taken us on our first trip to the animal shelter. But that visit had just been a tour. This time we were actually going to help out.

Everyone settled into their seats and grew quiet as Miss Chien, our teacher, greeted the class and walked to the front of the room.

"Please take out your math books," she said.

There was a low rumble as people reluctantly fumbled the fat textbooks out of their desks and set them on top, flipping the pages open to last week's work. Miss Chien wheeled out the overhead projector. "Okay, you know the drill. Pass your workbook to the person to your right, and we'll check the answers to last week's work." Miss Chien has a soft voice, which somehow manages to ring out across the room.

I flipped open my workbook and handed it to Jake, who sat to my right. Then I took the workbook from the girl on my left. My eyes went to the answers on the screen pulled down over the blackboard, then down to the page in front of me. I made the first tick with my pencil.

Would we get to walk the dogs, I wondered. Tick. It would be so cool if we got to walk the dogs. Tick.

"Conner." It was Miss Chien. Had she called me more than once? "Brianna's mark, please."

"Oh, yeah. Sorry." There were a few snickers as I quickly tallied up the marks on the page in front of me.

"Nine out of ten," I read out.

Miss Chien noted the mark in her record book and went on to the next person. I glanced at Jake. Had he already called out my mark?

Jake caught me looking, raised one eyebrow and tilted my workbook so I could see where he'd penciled in five out of ten. Not so good. I slumped back in my seat and waited for the rest of the marks to be read out.

Something knocked my foot, and I looked up as Jake's left leg withdrew under his seat.

"Boring," Jake mouthed when he'd caught my eye.

I nodded.

"Hand the books back now," Miss Chien was saying, "and we'll go over the questions you had trouble with."

There were several moments of shuffling as workbooks were returned. Before I could turn and take my book from Jake, he'd tossed it onto my desktop.

"Thanks a lot," I said.

I picked up the book and looked at the five X marks, sighed, then scanned the textbook until I found the first problem I'd gotten wrong. *If Alice knit a sweater out of two balls of wool, and each ball of wool was twenty-two meters long, how many centimeters of wool did Alice use?* I knew the problem was simple, but I couldn't get my mind around it. I tried to think of the numbers, but instead I kept picturing a ball of red wool lying on a carpet in a cozy living room. A fluffy black and white kitten leaped out from behind a chair and batted the ball of wool. The wool rolled across the carpet, and the kitten scampered after it. Maybe there'd be kittens at the animal shelter. No, probably not yet. Kittens were usually born in the spring, and that was a couple of months away yet.

"Conner, what about you?"

Startled, I looked up at Miss Chien.

"Are there any problems you'd like to go over?" Miss Chien asked.

I shook my head quickly and looked down at my desk. The eyes of the whole class were on me, making me wish I could disappear. If I needed to ask Miss Chien for help, I'd rather wait until after school than ask in front of the whole class.

A hand went up on the other side of the room, and Miss Chien turned.

"Can you go over question four?" Mercedes asked.

I shot her a grateful look. It was the wool question. I tried to concentrate on Miss Chien's words as she went over the problem step by step, writing out the numbers and equation on the blackboard. Finally, it made sense. But if they meant twenty-two multiplied by two multiplied by a hundred, why didn't they just say so? Who cared about a non-existent sweater and an imaginary ball of wool? Now, if the textbook writers had asked us to consider dogs . . .

If Conner walked his dog two blocks, and each block was twenty-two meters long, how many centimeters did Conner and his dog walk? Four thousand, four hundred centimeters. How long would that take with the dog stopping to sniff every few centimeters?

Reluctantly, I pulled my attention back to the classroom again. The rest of the day and two more whole days to go until the animal club meeting.

Disappointment

Wednesday afternoon finally arrived. The air was cold and the gray sky seemed close—as if snow might be on the way.

"Are you sure you don't want to come with us?" I said to Jake as we headed out of the school. Jake had his backpack slung over one shoulder and a basketball tucked under his other arm.

He shook his head. "Nah. Too many girls."

"If you came, there wouldn't be," I pointed out.

Jake shrugged and dropped his backpack at the edge of the school basketball court. He bounced the ball.

"Want to shoot a few hoops?" he asked.

"I don't have time." I could see Erika and Mercedes waving from Erika's dad's blue minivan. I hesitated beside the court, anxious to get going, but feeling things weren't quite right with Jake. I wished he could see how great the animal club was, but he never wanted to talk about it. He was a good friend to joke around with, but anything more serious than bike stuff and sports didn't seem to interest him.

"See ya later," I finally said.

I hurried to catch up to Erika and Mercedes. Annie Chang was there too, looking a bit impatient, her hands stuck deep in the pockets of her blue jacket. Mercedes was pulling on a pair of bright multicolored gloves. They matched the beads strung on strands of her long black hair, and her coat was bright red. I don't normally notice what girls are wearing, but Mercedes always stands out. Next to her, Annie and Erika looked kind of colorless. But Erika's smile was bright as I walked up to them.

We piled into the van, the three girls talking and giggling. The beads in Mercedes' hair clicked as she climbed into the backseat. I sat down quietly in the seat behind Mr. Leveson, feeling out of place. Maybe Jake had been right about there being too many girls. I wished Sean, the other guy in the club, had shown up today. Once we started driving, though, the girls calmed down.

"I wonder if we'll get to walk the dogs," Erika said from the seat beside me.

"I hope so," I told her.

I wondered if they ever got any Jack Russells at the shelter. It had been four days since the first rat sighting in our yard, and Dad hadn't caught anything in the trap he'd put out. I'd seen more droppings on the garbage can lid too, so the rat was still around.

"I asked my mom about getting a dog again," I said.

"Really?" Mercedes chimed in from the backseat. She and Annie stopped their conversation and leaned forward.

"What did she say?" Erika asked.

"No, as usual," I admitted, not able to keep the disappointment out of my voice.

The girls made sympathetic noises.

"But we do have one pet we weren't expecting," I said, trying to make a joke of it.

"Really?" said Erika.

"What?" Mercedes asked eagerly.

"A rat." Mom had told me not to talk about it, but I figured it was okay to tell the animal club.

"Ooo!" Annie said, wrinkling her nose. "You mean a real rat?"

"Yeah. I mean an uninvited one," I clarified.

I told them the story of what had happened on Saturday. They laughed at my description of Mom and the broom, but agreed that the right kind of dog might be good for keeping unwanted rats away.

"What about a cat?" Mercedes suggested. "Do you think they'd let you get a cat?"

"No, they don't want any pets," I said heavily. "Besides, even if they let me get a cat, I'd still be wishing I had a dog."

Erika smiled sympathetically.

"Well, you can visit my dogs any time you want," she said. Her eyes locked on mine for a moment.

"And you'll see plenty of dogs today at the shelter," Mercedes added.

Under her red coat, Mercedes was wearing a multi-colored shirt that she called her "lucky shirt." I wondered if maybe visiting the shelter meant as much to her as it did to me. She wasn't allowed to have pets either, but not because her parents didn't want any. Her apartment building didn't allow them.

The van pulled into the shelter's parking lot.

Mr. Leveson walked into the reception area with us and waited until a shelter worker came out to greet us. The woman, who was short and wide, introduced herself as Mini.

"I'll be back to pick you up around five o'clock," Erika's dad told us before turning to leave.

Mini looked us over. Her serious expression and the short military cut of her red hair made her appear severe and a bit intimidating.

But then she grinned and said, "All right. You're anxious to get to work, I can see."

We smiled back at her.

"Come on," she said, turning and gesturing for us to follow.

We walked past the reception desk, and Mini pushed open a door that led to the dog kennels. When the barking hit my ears, I felt a prickle of anticipation. A whole row of dogs in kennels was waiting, eager for attention. Would Mini assign each of us to a dog or would we get to pick our own dogs?

We stopped in the hallway on the other side of the door, and Mini pointed to the left.

"The dog kennels are down that way," she said.

"We know," Mercedes said. "We've been on a tour."

"Oh good, so you know your way around." Mini looked serious, but her eyes were smiling. "Then you know that the cat room and the small-animal room are down this way?" She waved a hand to the right.

We nodded.

"You can hang your coats here," she said, pointing to a row of hooks on the wall.

I took off my jacket and prepared to move toward the dog kennels.

"We're really glad you're here to help today," Mini said as she started walking in the opposite direction, obviously expecting us to follow.

I hesitated, meeting Erika's eyes. She shrugged and motioned with her head that we should follow Mini.

Reluctantly, I turned away from the kennels.

"We had a big seizure of small animals earlier this week. Mice, rats, gerbils, a rabbit. You name it. I think the pet store was only keeping the rats and mice alive to feed them to some big expensive snakes."

"That's awful," Erika said.

"Snakes need to eat too," Mini pointed out. "But you can't be cruel to the animals just because they're going to become snake food. The conditions they were living in were not good, and being fed alive to snakes is not a humane way to die." I looked at her, feeling confused.

"Don't we get to walk the dogs?" Mercedes asked.

Mini stopped in front of a glass-windowed door and turned back to us.

"Our regular volunteers have already walked the dogs today," she said. "But we sure need some help with these guys."

She pushed open the door. Erika was right behind Mini, and I heard her gasp. When we'd come for our tour, the small-animal room had been almost empty. Now, as I came up behind Erika, I could see that the room beyond the door was piled almost to the ceiling with cages. Most of the cages were wire, but some had glass or Plexiglass sides like terrariums. As I followed Mini into the room, I saw that the cages held mice, rats and assorted other small animals. My heart sank.

Rats. Instead of spending an afternoon with dogs, I was going to be spending it with a room full of dirty creepy rodents.

A scuffling sound in a cage beside me caught my attention, and I turned to look into the bead-like black eyes of a brown and white rat. It stood on its back legs, its forepaws held up over its chest, its nose twitching. I could see its long yellow teeth. In the next cage, two white rats clutched the bars of their cage with pink paws like little human hands. I repressed a shiver.

Someone slapped me on the back, and I jumped.

"I didn't like them at first either," Mini said with a laugh, her voice loud in the small room. "They made me nervous. Those mice move so quickly." She gestured to a cage in which two mice were running together on a squeaking wheel. A third mouse had just scampered up to the roof of its cage and hung there upside down.

"And those tails…" she added with a fake shudder.

I bent to peer into a cage where several rats slept, one on top of the other, their long, bare, scaly tails entwined.

"I always thought those tails were creepy," Mini said. "I was actually kind of scared of the rats," she admitted, "but I'm starting to find them quite lovely."

Lovely? It wasn't the word I would have chosen. But, I had to admit, they weren't as scary as I'd imagined when I discovered we had one in our yard. They were even kind of interesting.

"You know the saying 'dirty rat'?" Mini went on. "Well, it's not true. Rats are much cleaner than people realize." She pointed to a rat that was licking its paws and rubbing them over its fur. "Like little cats."

"What's this one?" Mercedes asked. The animal she pointed to looked something like a brown rat, but its body was rounder and its nose wasn't pointy. I couldn't see if it had a tail.

"That's a degu," Mini said. "They're originally from South America—the Andes I think. Whoever first brought them to North America thought they'd make good pets, but they don't. I'm sure they'd rather be back in their mountain burrows. This one bites, so be careful."

"What do you need us to do?" Erika asked, stepping forward.

"I need you to hold the animals while I clean their cages." Mini gestured to the soggy shredded newspaper at the bottom of one of the cages.

Mini opened the top of the cage beside me and reached inside. She withdrew her hands, gripping the brown and white rat around its middle.

"Here," she said, plunking the rat down on my chest. "You hold this one. I call him Oscar." I felt a flash of panic. I didn't want the rat on me. Despite my fear, my hands automatically rose to stop him from falling off. At the same time, I could feel his tiny claws digging through the fabric of my shirt, getting a grip of his own. Beneath my hands, his fur was soft, but a little coarse. His body felt warm, and I could feel his heart beating. I relaxed slightly.

Then the rat started climbing toward my head, and I felt another stab of panic. Horror movie images of vicious killer rats leapt into my mind. I looked to Erika for help, but Mini was loading a rat from a second cage into her arms.

"Don't worry. They're very friendly," Mini said, as if guessing my thoughts. "They're just curious. Their eyesight isn't so good, but their sense of smell is, so they're going to want to sniff you."

I pulled my rat down where I could get a better look at him. His nose and whiskers were twitching like crazy. His face was grayish brown, his nose slightly pink. I noticed for the first time that his whiskers were kinked—as if he'd stuck a paw in a light socket and gotten zapped. I looked over at the rat Erika was holding. Its whiskers were completely straight. I turned back to Oscar and noticed that his ears stuck out a bit at the sides of his head, too. Perhaps he was a bit of a rat oddball. He seemed to be looking right into my eyes. His twitching nose reached up.

"Hi, Oscar," I said, feeling a bit foolish. I glanced up to see if the others had noticed I'd started talking to a rat, but they were all busy with rats of their own. Mercedes seemed to be having a genuine conversation with hers.

"Oh, hold still!" Annie told her rat as it tried to escape her grasp. It popped out of her hands for a moment, like a slippery bar of soap. Annie squeaked and caught it again.

Mini was grinning as she pulled the wad of disintegrated newspaper out of the first cage—careful to lift it by its dry corners—and stuffed it into a large black garbage bag. She did the same for the second cage.

"We change the food and water every day," she explained, "and everything else—lock, stock and barrel— three times a week. We scrub the bottoms of the cages, wash the food and water dishes, put in clean newspaper and fresh wood shavings."

She placed a new layer of newspaper into each cage and poured some wood shavings over that; then she replaced the rat toys, the little cardboard houses, the hiding-tubes and the food dishes, which she must have removed and washed before we got there.

"Okay," she said. "You can put those guys back in now."

Oscar had climbed up to my right shoulder and was sitting comfortably tucked in under my ear.

"Hey, I think he likes you," Mini said.

I grinned, pleased. Carefully, I lifted the rat off my shoulder, feeling surprisingly reluctant to put him back in the cage. I held him in my hands for a moment, and he poked his head out between my fingers and stared at me.

"You've gotta go back now, Oscar," I told him as I lifted him up to the cage. I reached in through the open cage top, and Oscar leapt from my hands. As I pulled away, he scurried to the top of the cardboard house, stood on his hind legs and stretched up his pointy nose. It was almost as if he were trying to get closer to me, or at least get a better look. Maybe he really did like me.

"Wait! Not in that cage," Mini said as Mercedes started to put her rat in with Oscar. "We don't want to mix the males and the females or we'll have even more rats to look after."

"Oops, sorry," Mercedes said, quickly shifting her white rat to the next cage. "There you go, Lacy," she crooned as she let the rat go.

Erika's and Annie's rats followed Lacy.

"Why is Oscar by himself?" I asked Mini.

"Boys don't always get along," she explained. "But the girls like to socialize," she added with a wink at me.

We moved on to the next cages, and I glanced back at Oscar, alone in his cage, his nose pointed after me, his twisted whiskers twitching.

Trapped

After we'd finished sweeping out the small-animal room, Mini let us go, saying we could come back again on Friday if we wanted to.

"Hey!" she called out, following us to the reception area. "If any of you want to foster one or two of the small animals, that would be a big help. Ask your parents."

"Foster?" Mercedes asked.

"Take them home and look after them for a while," Mini explained. "The small-animal room is overcrowded, and it would make my job easier if some of the animals were fostered out."

"How long would we get to keep them?" Erika asked.

"Two weeks—maybe a bit longer. By then we'll know if the SPCA is getting custody of the animals."

"What do you mean by custody?" Mercedes asked, voicing my questions as usual.

"When we get custody, the animals become ours, and we can adopt them out to permanent homes," explained Mini.

"What about the pet store?" I asked.

"The court case will decide."

"Court case?" It was Annie this time.

"You kids sound like parrots," Mini said with a frown. Annie reddened, and Mini's eyes laughed again.

"Oh, don't worry about it," she said. "I like it when people ask questions. Better than having them shut up and pretend they know something when they don't. You want to know why there's a court case? It's because we're charging that pet store with cruelty to animals."

Her last words dropped like a judge's gavel, and there was a moment of silence.

"We?" Mercedes asked.

"The SPCA," Mini explained. "The Society for the Prevention of Cruelty to Animals."

We all nodded.

"There are laws against being cruel to animals, you know," Mini continued. "And we want to make sure people obey those laws. We give them a chance to improve things, and if they don't, we charge them with cruelty."

Mini's face was hard, and she looked ready to personally take on anyone who dared to hurt an animal. Then she grinned again.

"I think your ride's here," she said, pointing out the window to where Erika's dad's van was pulling into the parking lot.

"So, I'll see you all on Friday?" she asked as we pulled on our coats and headed for the door.

"Sure, we'll be here," we chorused, a little afraid to say anything else.

In the van, everyone began talking at once.

"Rats are so cool," Mercedes said.

"Dad, can we foster a rat?" Erika asked.

"Rats? I thought you were going to be walking dogs and petting cats," Mr. Leveson said with a laugh.

"I didn't really like the rats," Annie cut in. "The hamster and the rabbit were cuter."

"But all the hamster did was sleep," Erika said.

She was right. The one hamster, in a cage all by itself, had stayed in a round furry ball, fast asleep the whole time, barely waking even when it had been lifted out for its cage cleaning.

"Mini said that hamsters are nocturnal," Mercedes pointed out. "They get active at night and sleep all day."

"Aren't rats nocturnal too?" I asked.

"Maybe," Erika said. "Some of them were sleeping when we first went in."

"Well, the ones I had to hold weren't sleeping!" Annie said. She gave a shudder. "And I still hate their tails."

The rest of us laughed. Soon the van pulled up in front of my house, and I climbed out, thanking Erika's dad for the ride. I walked around to the back of the house and paused at the bottom of the stairs to check the rat trap Dad had set out behind the garbage can. Empty. I was relieved. It was too weird to think I'd actually been holding a rat just fifteen minutes ago. Was there any point in asking Mom and Dad if I could foster one? I looked at the empty rat trap again and had to laugh. A rat in the house? Not likely.

Still, I was in a good mood as I ran up the back stairs. I paused at the door. The muted sound of piano music came from inside the house. So much for my good mood. Jenna was practicing, and it would be my turn next.

"Hi, Mom," I said as I came through the door into the kitchen and began taking off my shoes. She was standing at the counter, starting supper. I glanced at the chicken-shaped clock that hung on the wall above the kitchen table. Quarter after five already. Dad would be home around six from his job at the bank.

"Hello there. How was your day?" Mom asked, glancing up from a tray of what looked like pork chops. She was covering them with some kind of sauce. Since joining the animal club, I'd started to feel a bit weird about eating animals and had been trying to eat vegetarian whenever I could. Some days Mom actually cooked a vegetarian meal for us, but this obviously wasn't one of those days. Maybe tonight I could eat cheese instead.

"Good," I said, ignoring the pork chops. "We went to the animal shelter after school."

"Hmm." Mom nodded as she lifted the tray and turned to open the oven door.

I waited for her to ask me about the shelter, but she didn't.

"I'm going to do some homework," I told her.

"Okay, dear." She was back at the counter, focusing on food again. "Don't forget to wash your hands."

I made a face, which she didn't notice, then headed for the bathroom. Passing the door to the living room, I caught a glimpse of Jenna sitting straight-backed at the piano, her brownish black hair pulled into a ponytail. There hadn't been a pause in her playing since I'd entered the house. The sounds that Bach or Mozart had imagined two or three hundred years ago poured from the piano. They probably wouldn't mind hearing Jenna play their music, but they'd be rolling in their graves as soon as I got to the keys.

In my room, I closed the door behind me and went straight to my desk. I turned on my radio to a rock music station, then pulled *The Complete Guide to Dogs* off the shelf above my desk, not wanting to think about piano and not ready to face homework. I flipped idly through the pages, my mind not focusing on the dogs as intently as it usually did.

At the Terrier section I stopped and read:

Terriers have always enjoyed a close relationship with farmers, for whom they have worked tirelessly, killing rats and other vermin... Their strong, locking jaws and sharp teeth were powerful weapons against animals fighting for their lives.

I pictured Oscar's trusting grayish brown face and twitching nose. Suddenly, a Jack Russell terrier did not sound as appealing as it had earlier. I flipped back to the section on Retrievers. The Labrador retriever. Now there was a nice dog. A Lab mix like Erika's dog Jenny—that's the kind of dog I wanted. The kind of dog that would be a real friend. A dog I could adopt from the shelter.

I tried to conjure up the old daydream of me running beside a beautiful chocolate-colored Lab, but my mind was still clamoring with images from earlier in the afternoon. Piles of cages. Rats, mice, the degu, hamsters, a big white rabbit ...the prick of tiny rat claws on my skin, the feel of Oscar's small body in my hands, the beating of his heart through his warm coarse fur.

"Conner!" Jenna's voice, muffled by my closed door, interrupted my thoughts.

I turned down the radio.

"What?"

"I'm finished with the piano, and Mom says you're supposed to practice before supper," Jenna said.

"I'll be there in a minute," I told her; then I turned the radio up again and returned to the dog book.

I tried to read a bit more, but couldn't muster my old enthusiasm. My mind returned to the afternoon at the shelter, replaying my encounter with Oscar and the other animals. I guess way more than one minute passed. There was a sharp knock on my door, then it opened. I turned, ready to get mad at Jenna, but it was Dad. He was dressed in his work clothes—dark suit, shirt and tie—and he wasn't smiling.

"Dad! I didn't hear you come home," I said, quickly switching off the radio and closing my book.

His thick black eyebrows lowered.

"Your mother says you were called to practice the piano twenty minutes ago," he said gravely.

I cringed inwardly.

"Sorry, Dad. I lost track of time."

"Well, you can do ten minutes now and the rest after supper."

"Okay, Dad," I said without enthusiasm.

I got slowly to my feet. Dad waited for me by the door, his face softening. As I passed him he smiled and reached out to tousle my hair.

"Don't worry," he said. "Keep practicing, and some day you'll be as good as your sister."

I rolled my eyes.

"I'll never be as good as Jenna," I mumbled. "I don't even want to be."

But Dad didn't seem to hear. As far as he was concerned, I was going to play the piano, I was going to be good at it and I was going to like it. He refused to believe anything else.

C D E F G A B C. My shoulders slumped as I anticipated the monotony of practicing scales.

I paused in the hall and turned back to Dad.

"Have you ever heard of Chinese water torture?" I asked over my shoulder.

"What?"

I sighed. He'd never understand.

"Oh, nothing," I said as I headed to the living room.

As I sat down at the piano bench, the image of the rat trap under the stairs snapped into my mind.

Snow

The next day I woke up to discover that snow covered the ground. It probably wouldn't last, but I wouldn't be able to take my bike to school.

"I might not be here when you get home after school," Mom announced at breakfast. "Julie and I are catering a conference next weekend, and we're going to be doing a lot of preparation over the next few days."

Julie was Mom's partner in her catering business. Mom worked at home most days and did a lot of her food preparation there, but when a special event came up, she might disappear with Julie for a day or two, picking up supplies and cooking at Julie's house. Julie didn't have any family, so it was easier for them to take over her kitchen to prepare for a bigger event.

"Here, I need you to be guinea pigs," Mom said, setting a tray on the table in front of Jenna and me. Dad had already left for work.

"I made these last night," Mom explained. "They're called Galloping Horses."

I thought about the term "guinea pig" as I warily eyed the tiny pastry cups filled with an unidentifiable brown mixture. Guinea pigs, like rats and rabbits, were animals that scientists used in experiments. Testing products on animals was one of the topics the animal club had discussed already. I thought of Mrs. Ferguson's classroom guinea pig, Daisy—the long white fur that hid her face, the gentle squeaking sound she made when the little kids stroked her back. I hated the thought of anyone experimenting on her.

"They're an appetizer," Mom was saying. "It's just a bit of pork, onions, chopped peanuts . . ." She looked hurt when neither of us appeared eager to try the things on the tray.

Finally Jenna reached out and gingerly took a pastry cup.

"What's that on top?" she asked, looking at the thing in her hand with suspicion.

"It's just a piece of pineapple," Mom said, suddenly impatient. "Hurry up. You're going to be late for school, and I need to know what you think."

The pineapple wasn't what concerned me, but I decided not to complain about the meat this time. Bracing myself for the worst, I grabbed one of the horse things and stuffed it in my mouth. The taste was a mix of spicy, savory and sweet.

"They're good," Jenna said.

"Yah," I agreed unintelligibly, my mouth full.

"Honestly, I don't know why you're so surprised," Mom complained. "Isn't my cooking always delicious?"

"Always," Jenna said, grabbing another appetizer off the tray and beaming at Mom as she bounced up from the table. Mom smiled back, and I felt a twinge of annoyance. Everything Jenna said or did pleased Mom.

I swallowed my Galloping Horse mouthful and tried to think of something impressive that I could add.

"*Magnifique*," I said, trying to sound like a fancy French chef.

"What did you say, Conner?" Mom asked.

"Oh nothing." I sighed and headed for the back door to get my running shoes and jacket.

"Your French needs some work," Jenna whispered as she leaned past me to pull on her boots.

"Shut up!" I snapped, a little too loudly.

"Conner!" Mom exclaimed. "Don't talk to your sister like that."

"She started it," I protested.

"I don't care who started it," Mom went on. "You two should be able to get along for one morning."

I gritted my teeth to keep from saying anything more and busied myself with putting on my running shoes.

"Don't you have any boots?" Mom asked. "Your feet are going to get wet."

"My boots are too small. I'll be fine," I said, shouldering my backpack and opening the back door.

"I'll take you to buy boots as soon as this catering job is finished," Mom said as she turned back to the kitchen.

Once Mom's back was turned, Jenna pushed by me, her bulky backpack and violin case bumping against my side.

"Watch it," I hissed, keeping my voice low.

"Thanks for holding the door, little brother," she said in a fake-sweet voice as she flounced down the stairs.

Gritting my teeth with frustration, I stepped after Jenna just as Mom came up behind me. She caught the door before I could close it and leaned out after us.

"Be careful on the stairs," she called. "They're slippery."

I rolled my eyes. Why did it feel like the warning was only for me? I couldn't even go down a bunch of ordinary steps without Mom thinking she had to give me directions.

Jenna was already off the last step and disappearing around the corner of the house when my foot slipped. I grabbed for the stair railing and caught myself just in time.

"And watch out for that rat," Mom called after me.

Despite my annoyance, I had to smile. Did she expect the rat to leap out and ambush me at the bottom of the stairs?

On the last step I craned my head around the corner and looked at the garbage can. It was covered in white, like a big iced cookie. There were no marks, no footprints.

"No sign of it," I called up to Mom.

"Oh, good," she said, relief in her voice. "Maybe the snow chased it away."

"Maybe," I said, hoping it was true and hoping there wasn't a dead rat in the trap under the snow.

At school I was greeted by a snowball in the face. I wiped the cold stuff from my eyes and caught sight of Jake by the school-ground fence, raising his arm for another throw. His face looked dark against the snow, and his eyes seemed narrowed. For a second I wondered if he was mad at me, but there was no time to think or to protest. I ducked quickly, reaching down to grab a handful of snow at the same time. My retaliating snowball exploded across Jake's jacket front. The war was on.

Snowballs flew back and forth. Finally, laughing and covered with snow, we called a truce as the buzzer rang, signalling us to go inside.

"You're not supposed to throw snowballs on the school grounds," a little kid said as she hurried by us, her pale face barely visible between a large red toque and a thick blue scarf.

Jake and I looked at each other and laughed. But still, there was a tiny tug of uncertainty somewhere inside me. Had the snowball fight been just for fun? Or had there been something else behind Jake's attack?

By lunch break, I had forgotten my concern. The snow was still on the ground, and Jake and I joined a group of kids rolling snowballs to make a fort. As usual, the lunch-hour monitors were on patrol, which meant no one could get away with throwing snowballs. Some grade one and two kids were seeing how big a snowball they could roll. When it got too large for them to push, they asked for our help. There wasn't much snow on the ground, so as we rolled the ball along, it began to pick up bits of rock and dirt from the gravel field under the snow. By the end of lunch hour, the field was mostly bare gray with a few large, dirty snowballs stranded in the middle of it.

By Friday it was raining and there was nothing left of the snow except a few fast-melting mounds. After school I was glad to get a ride to the animal shelter from Erika's dad. I was surprised to find I was even looking forward to seeing the rats again.

Volunteers

We stepped into the small animal room and into the musty stink of animal bodies, urine and feces. The place definitely needed our help.

"Why don't you two take the rats," Mini said, pointing at Erika and me. "And you two"—she nodded at Mercedes and Annie—"can start over there." She gestured toward the rabbit cage, then handed out garbage bags to all of us.

"Well, what are you waiting for?" she barked as none of us moved.

Annie wrinkled her nose. Erika and I looked at each other, took a deep breath and started forward.

"Let's start with Oscar," I suggested.

As we approached his cage, Oscar scurried up to the roof of his cardboard house, sniffing the air.

"One of us should hold him while the other cleans the cage," Erika said.

"Okay," I agreed.

There was a pause. It was obvious we both wanted the holding job. Finally, Erika sighed.

"Go ahead," she said resignedly. "I'll clean this one if you do the next."

I grinned at her and reached for the door on top of the cage. Oscar stretched his nose up to sniff my hand. Did he recognize me? I let him smell my fingers for a few seconds, then scratched the soft fur under his chin. He seemed to like it.

With both hands I took hold of Oscar's small furry body and lifted him out of the cage.

"It's all yours," I said to Erika.

"Thanks. Thanks a lot," she grumbled as she lifted the top off the cage, but I could tell she was joking.

I held Oscar against my chest, making a ledge for him to sit on with my left arm while I petted him with the other hand. He crawled along my arm to my wrist and poked his nose into the sleeve of my sweatshirt. His whiskers tickled.

Erika unclamped the metal top of Oscar's cage and lifted it off the plastic cage bottom, then tilted the bottom section to dump the old wood shavings and damp newspaper bedding into her garbage bag. After that she washed and refilled the food and water dishes.

"Did any of you ask your parents about fostering one of the animals?" Mini asked as she looked over our work.

"Mine said yes," Annie and Erika said at once.

"No pets allowed at our place," Mercedes said, looking down at the floor, her voice glum. Then she looked up and grinned.

"We haven't asked our landlord yet, but my parents think he won't mind me having one small caged animal if it's only for a few weeks," she added triumphantly. She'd been faking the gloominess.

"That's great!" Erika told her.

"They think a rat might be pushing it, though," Mercedes admitted. "They said I should probably take a hamster."

"That's no problem," Mini said.

I looked down at Oscar. The others were so lucky. Why couldn't my parents be like theirs? I stroked the top of Oscar's head, wondering what it would be like to take care of him every day.

"What about you?" Mini asked, turning to me.

I felt a dull ache in my chest, knowing I had to admit I was the only one who wasn't allowed to foster a pet. Would one of the others take Oscar? The ache in my chest gave a little push, and before I realized what I was doing, my mouth opened and words leapt out.

"I can take Oscar."

What had I said?

"Really?" Erika was excited. "Your parents said yes?"

I shrugged, not meeting her eyes. I suddenly felt hot.

"They won't mind," I said, thinking quickly. Could I really take him? "I can keep him in my bedroom. They won't even know he's there."

Why not? It could work. Mom was catering that conference today. Dad wouldn't be home till later. I just had to get the cage past Jenna and into my room.

I barely heard what the others said after that. My hands were sweating and my head was whirling. Oscar ran up my arm, twitching his nose like crazy, as if he could sense something was up. Erika nudged me.

"You can put him back in now," she said, gesturing at Oscar's clean, restocked cage.

I set Oscar onto the fresh wood shavings, and Erika put the cage top back on, securing the clips. I looked the cage over, thinking hard. It was way too big to hide in my backpack, but if Jenna was still practicing the piano when I got home, she wouldn't notice anything. Once I got the cage in my room I could keep it on the floor where no one would see it from the door. I could hide it in my closet when I was out of my room and at school. Oscar wouldn't mind it in there, I hoped.

"Conner!" Erika nudged me again.

"Oh, sorry. What?"

"Your turn," she said with a wave at the cage with the three female white rats.

Oscar

After we finished at the shelter, Erika's dad drove us all home again. Beside me, Erika held the cage with the three white rats on her lap. In the backseat, Mercedes had the hamster and Annie had the rabbit. I had Oscar. I could hardly believe what I was doing.

"Thanks for the ride," I called over my shoulder as I climbed out of the van in front of my house. I hoped my nervousness didn't show.

As the van pulled away, I glanced stealthily left and right. No neighbors visible. No cars in the driveway in front of our house. No one in any of our windows. If anyone was looking, there would be no way of hiding Oscar's cage. Mom and Dad weren't home, and Jenna was probably practicing the piano, but if any of the neighbors saw me, they might say something to Mom or Dad. I hurried to the side gate, holding the cage between me and the house, hoping my body was at least partially shielding the cage from view.

Once I was behind the house, I relaxed a bit. At least the neighbors couldn't see me now. But the hardest part was yet to come. My sweating hands slipped on the handle of the cage, and I held on tighter as I climbed the stairs quickly but carefully. At the door to the kitchen, I paused to listen. Yes. There was the sound of the piano. I set the cage down while I fished out my key. Then I took a deep breath and opened the door.

My heart pounded like a drum as I stepped into the empty kitchen. Here I was in the middle of Mom's antiseptically clean kitchen, holding a rat. Mom would flip out if she knew. Now I just had to pass the open doorway to the living room where Jenna sat at the piano. Come on, I told myself. She won't even look up.

"Here we go," I whispered to Oscar as I shifted the cage to my left side, opposite the living room door, and headed for the hall to my room.

"Conner?"

My heart jumped, but I didn't stop until I'd passed the doorway. Had she seen me? Had she seen the cage?

"Is that you?" she asked, with no pause in her playing.

"Yeah." I poked my head back around the doorframe, keeping the cage out of sight in the hall. Did I sound natural or suspicious?

"You're supposed to set the table," Jenna said without looking at me. Her eyes stayed on the music book in front of her, and her fingers didn't even falter on the keys.

A prickle of annoyance ran up my neck. I wanted to throw something at the back of Jenna's head, make her mess up her playing. But I was hiding Oscar's cage, and I didn't want Jenna to turn around. Instead I gave her a one-handed salute that she didn't see.

"Aye, aye," I said as I continued down the hall. "As soon as I finish in my room."

I opened the door to my bedroom, stepped inside with Oscar's cage in my arms and closed the door behind us. We'd made it.

I set Oscar's cage down on top of my bed and sat down beside it on the blue duvet cover. I slipped off my backpack and dropped it beside me.

"This is my room," I said to Oscar, reaching a finger through the top bars of the cage. He stood up on his hind legs to sniff me.

We stayed like that for a few seconds; then I glanced over at the door. We were safe as long as I could hear Jenna practicing, but Mom and Dad would be home soon. I realized I'd better not leave Oscar's cage on the bed in full view. I shifted the cage to the floor, where it couldn't be seen unless someone walked right into the room. Then I went to check out my closet.

The closet floor wasn't too bad—a couple of pairs of shoes, some crumpled pieces of paper, a broken model of the *Millennium Falcon*, a few loose Lego pieces and a shirt that had fallen off a hanger. I hung up the shirt, put away the Lego bits, tossed out the papers and kicked the shoes into the far corner of the closet.

"Okay, Oscar," I said as I picked up the cage again. "I hope you're not afraid of the dark."

I bent down to place the cage on the carpet in the closet and slid it as far in as it would go. Then I went back to my bed to get Oscar's supplies out of my pack. The wood shavings had a pungent smell even through the plastic bag. I stuffed the bag into the back corner of the closet with the shoes, hoping Mom wouldn't notice the smell if she came into my room. I checked Oscar's water dish. Some of the water had slopped out during the move. "I'll be back in a minute," I told Oscar, then crept out to the washroom with his dish.

Back in my room, I placed the dish of fresh water in Oscar's cage, then reached inside the cage to lift him out, wanting to give him a bit of exercise while I had the chance. I looked at my bedroom floor, then at the shelves, the dresser, the desk, the bed—there were too many things he could hide under if he decided to make a run for it. Better put him on the bed.

"There you go," I said, setting him down in the middle of the duvet.

He immediately ran for the edge of the bed. When he saw how sharply it dropped off, he scurried back to check out the opposite edge. Next he ran for the pillow end of the bed, which must have looked like a mountain to him. He nudged around at the bottom end of the pillow as if searching for something. Was he looking for a place to hide? Maybe he was scared out in the open.

I sank to my knees beside the bed and pulled on the duvet cover so that it bunched up to make a kind of trench that almost touched at the top. Oscar immediately ran for it, ducking in between the folds of fabric. He paused for a second, sniffing, then moved through the trench as if exploring. His tail and a bit of his back fur poked out between the folds of duvet.

I looked around my room for something else I could add to Oscar's play area. With a flash of inspiration, I grabbed *The Complete Guide to Dogs* off my desk, then sat down on the bed and smoothed out the duvet cover. At once Oscar began to search around for a place to hide. Quickly, I opened the book to the middle and flipped it upside down on the bed so that it sat with its spine sticking up and its sides making a kind of tent. Oscar scurried up to sniff the book, then darted in between the open pages and settled there. When I peeked under the book, he was sitting back on his hind legs, grooming himself.

Thud, thud. I jumped as someone knocked on my bedroom door. I suddenly realized that I could no longer hear the piano. At that moment the door opened, and Jenna's face peered around it.

"Hey!" I protested. My heart thumped, but I stopped myself from throwing my arms out to hide Oscar. That would only draw attention to him. Calmly, I turned my back on Oscar and faced Jenna, telling myself to act natural. Oscar was hidden under the book. Jenna wouldn't even see him.

Stay under there, Oscar. I willed him not to move.

"I told you, you're supposed to set the table," Jenna said. "I've already put the supper in the oven, and Mom and Dad will be home any minute. And you haven't practiced, either."

Even if I'd wanted to practice, how was I supposed to with her hogging the piano? But I bit back the comment. I didn't want an argument. I wanted her to go away.

"All right, I'm coming now," I said. "You can go."

Jenna glared at me for a second, then disappeared, banging the door shut behind her.

I let my breath out with relief. That was a close one.

Quickly, I lifted away *The Complete Guide to Dogs* and scooped up Oscar.

"Sorry, guy," I told him. "I've got to put you back in your cage for now."

I carried Oscar back to his cage and dropped some dry food into his food dish before closing the top of the cage. I really hoped he didn't mind staying in the closet. If rats were nocturnal, he wouldn't mind the dark, would he? Or would it confuse him to be in the dark when it wasn't night? I'd have to look for a book about rats. There was a lot I didn't know about them.

I stood up, feeling a wave of elation. It was only temporary, and it wasn't a dog, but at least I had a pet. This was going to be great!

Announcement

"Now, let's hear how you're coming with the minuet," Miss Remple said as she leaned over me.

I heard her take a sip of coffee, and I flipped quickly through the pages of my music book. I wasn't in a hurry to play the minuet, but at least the notes would cover up the gulping gurgle of her swallow. I found the page, pressed the book open and readied my fingers over the keys.

Too late. Once again I tried not to shudder as my imagination followed the progress of the coffee down Miss Remple's throat. I tried to block out her presence by concentrating on the music, but instead I thought about Oscar.

How was he making out in the closet? Was he sleeping? Was he wondering where I was? Was Mom discovering him right this very moment?

My fingers fumbled on the piano keys and I hit a succession of wrong notes.

"I think you'd better start from the beginning again," Miss Remple said. Her voice sounded tight, as if it was taking some effort to keep exasperation out of it, but I could still feel it in the air. I didn't blame her for being fed up with my playing, though. I was too. We'd both be happier if Mom and Dad would just let me quit.

I started the piece again, trying to keep my mind on what I was doing. This time I made it through with only a couple of small mistakes, which Miss Remple over-looked.

"All right," she said. "I think that's enough for today."

I sighed with relief and eagerly closed my book. It wouldn't be long now until I was back at home checking on Oscar.

"Just one more thing," Miss Remple said, halting me as I headed for the door. "We've got a recital coming up next month. I'd like you to work on getting the minuet perfect by then."

I stifled a groan.

"A recital?"

"Don't look so worried," she said with a smile. "It's just a small event—an opportunity for my students to perform for their families. I won't assign you anything new to prepare, so there should be no pressure. You had the minuet well in hand last week. I'm not sure what happened today. Three weeks should give you plenty of time to learn to play it with complete confidence."

It may have been my imagination, but she didn't look like she believed that. I know I didn't.

Then I remembered the bike competition. That was next month too. The competition was on February 10. The recital couldn't possibly be on the same day, could it?

"Miss Remple?" I asked apprehensively. "What date is the recital?"

"It'll be on the second Saturday—the tenth, I think."

My heart sank. How could I possibly be in two places at once?

"In the morning?" I asked hopefully. The bike competition was in the afternoon. Maybe if I couldn't get out of the recital, I could still make it to the competition.

Miss Remple nodded.

"We'll start at 10:30," she said. "We should be finished by noon."

"That's great," I exclaimed, giving her a big grin.

She smiled back.

"Do you have something else happening that day?"

"A bike competition," I said. I hadn't meant to tell her, but in my relief I blurted it out.

"Hmm," she said, giving me a considering look. "What kind of bike competition?"

"Ah…" I stalled, feeling my face coloring. Miss Remple was my piano teacher. She probably thought bike stunts were stupid or uncouth or something. I looked at the door, anxious to get going, but Miss Remple was waiting for me to say more.

"BMX stunts," I told her.

Miss Remple raised her eyebrows.

"That sounds very intriguing," she said. "And that's in the afternoon?"

"Yeah," I said, pulling on my coat. "I better get going now."

Miss Remple stood at the door, watching me get on my bike. As I put pavement between us, Miss Remple and piano lessons quickly dropped from my mind. I wanted to get straight home to Oscar, but I had one quick detour to make on the way. I needed a book about rats.

It didn't take long to pedal to the public library, and I was in and out in about ten minutes. Without slowing down, I stuffed the book in my backpack and hopped back on my bike.

I pedaled the rest of the way home at full speed, anxiety adding energy to my legs. I'd hung a *Keep Out* sign on my bedroom door and assured Mom that my room was clean, but you never knew with Mom. If she decided the whole house needed vacuuming or disinfecting or something, no sign would keep her out.

I parked my bike in the garage and took the back steps two at a time. Oscar was probably wondering where I was by now. Maybe he was hungry. I'd only left a small amount of food in his dish because it was more fun to feed it to him by hand. I slowed down as I opened the door to the house. What if Mom had found Oscar? What if she'd freaked out and thumped him with the broom, like she'd tried to do to the rat in the yard?

My chest felt tight as I stepped into the kitchen. Dad was standing by the stove, and I could smell something cooking. What was he doing here? On Saturday morning he was usually out doing errands or playing golf. Then I remembered that Mom was catering the conference this weekend.

"Hi." Dad turned to me and smiled. "You're just in time. I'm heating up some soup."

I grinned back, relieved. Mom was away, and Dad had probably not gone anywhere near my bedroom.

"How was piano?" Dad asked as I hung up my coat and slipped off my shoes.

My chest tightened once again as I remembered the upcoming recital.

"Good," I said, adjusting my coat on the hook and not looking at him. Maybe if I didn't mention the recital, Dad and Mom wouldn't find out about it. Maybe I could avoid the recital altogether and just go to the bike competition.

"Jenna says you've got a recital coming up," Dad said.

My hopes sank. I'd forgotten about Jenna. She also took lessons with Miss Remple, so of course she'd know about the recital. For a second I considered trying to persuade Dad that the recital was only for students at Jenna's level, but I knew Jenna would tell him the truth, so I just nodded.

"That's great," Dad said, grinning enthusiastically and not noticing I wasn't. "Your mom and I are really looking forward to it."

Yeah, just great. I gave my shoes a light kick to move them out of the way of the door, suppressing the urge to kick them a lot harder. I wished I could get Mom and Dad to understand that I hated playing the piano. Just the thought of sitting down at the piano in front of a bunch of people made me feel sick. Even if I could play the minuet without butchering it, I'd feel sick.

"Do I have to do the recital?" I asked, a note of pleading creeping into my voice.

"Of course," Dad said. He opened a cupboard door and lifted out bowls and side plates, then turned to me. "The recital is your opportunity to showcase the results of all that hard work you've put in. Haven't you been practicing hard?"

"Yeah, but—"

"Well, then. You've got nothing to worry about. I'm sure we'll be proud of both you and Jenna."

I opened my mouth to protest further, but Dad had that unbendable look on his face. Now was probably not the time to tell him about the bike competition either. He'd likely think I just wanted to get out of the recital to do bike stuff, which, to him, was like watching television instead of doing homework. Besides, I really wanted to get away and check on Oscar. I mumbled something that sounded like agreement. Dad looked satisfied and turned his attention to the pot on the stove.

"Lunch is in five minutes," he said as he stirred the pot.

I headed out of the kitchen, feeling trapped again.

"And Conner," Dad called after me. "Mom left some new clothes outside your door. Make sure you put them away. They're for Chinese New Year."

I'd forgotten that Chinese New Year was almost here. At least I could look forward to dinner at Yeh Yeh and Ma Ma's house (Yeh Yeh and Ma Ma are what Jenna and I call Grandma and Grandpa Lee, our Cantonese grandparents). I like seeing my cousin Ryan and the other relatives I don't see very often, and of course I like getting lucky money. But I'd give up all my lucky money if it could get me out of the recital.

Close Call

At my bedroom door I bent down to pick up the pile of neatly folded clothes, my thoughts anxiously jumping to Oscar again. I hadn't seen Jenna this morning. Would she have gone into my room? Was Oscar all right?

I opened the door and quickly tossed the new clothes and my backpack onto the bed, closing the door behind me. Looking around, I saw nothing out of place. There was no sign that anyone had been in the room, and nothing gave away Oscar's presence.

The room was silent.

I felt a sudden stab of panic. Whenever we walked into Mrs. Ferguson's classroom to feed Daisy the guinea pig, she always squeaked her excitement. But I'd never heard Oscar make a sound. Was he still here? Was he okay?

In two strides I crossed the room and opened the closet door. Light fell over Oscar's cage, which sat on the floor just as I'd left it. In the middle of the cage, Oscar stood on his hind legs as if waiting for me.

"Hey, Oscar," I greeted him, a wave of relief washing over me. Keeping a rat hidden in my room was turning out to be more stressful than I'd imagined.

I opened the cage and stuck in my hand, letting Oscar sniff my fingers before I stroked the fur on his nose and back.

"Are you hungry, Oscar?"

I pulled my hand out of the cage and found the container of dry food. There were pellets that looked like dog food, Cheerios, nuts and other cereal-type things. I selected one of the Cheerios, and Oscar stretched up eagerly to take it from my fingers. He held the Cheerio in his forepaws while he chewed, making quick work of it. I passed him a pellet next, and it too disappeared. When I handed him a nut, he took it from my fingers, ran into his cardboard house, stashed it, then popped back out to see what I'd give him next. I laughed. I passed him another nut, and he stashed that too. Again, he scurried back out and stood up, expectantly. I tried another piece of cereal, and he hid that too.

I suddenly realized that I was laughing out loud and clamped my mouth shut. I'd forgotten all about Dad, and Jenna might be home too. I'd even forgotten to worry about the recital and everything else to do with piano. I stood back and listened for a moment, but there were no sounds outside my bedroom door. I heard a muffled call from the kitchen. Lunch must be ready.

I knelt back down by Oscar's cage and secured the cage door.

"I've got to go for lunch now, Oscar," I whispered. "But I won't be long. I'll try to bring you back something good to eat," I added.

I turned to go, leaving the closet door open so that he'd have some light. I figured it was safe, since everyone would be in the kitchen. I glanced at my backpack on the bed. I'd almost forgotten about the rat book. Maybe I could just take a quick peek inside.

I slipped the small book, titled *Rats: A Pet Owner's Manual,* out of my backpack and sat down on the bed, opening to the first page.

> *The ancestors of all rats kept as house pets today are brown rats* (Rattus norvegicus). *Two hundred years ago they came to Europe from China. Brown rats came to North America as stowaways on ships, hidden among the cargo in the eighteenth century.*

Interesting. I looked over at Oscar sitting in his cage. Even though he was grayish brown and white, he was descended from a brown rat whose ancestors came from Asia, just like half of mine did.

> *When living among humans, brown rats live close to the ground, inhabiting basements of houses and frequently sewers.*

So the brown rat was the sewer rat everyone hated—

probably the same kind of rat that had been in our yard. I flipped ahead in the book, checking out the headings: Food, Housing, Health, Behavior. I'd have to read through everything more carefully later. I stopped flipping when a heading caught my eye. Training.

Using food as a reward almost always guarantees that a pet rat will learn what you want to teach it.

Cool. I hadn't thought about that. Maybe I could train Oscar to do some tricks, just like you can train a dog. I could get him to come when I called him or—

Suddenly there was a knock, and the door to my room opened. I looked up with a start, dropping the rat book on the bed. Dad's face peered in at me, his expression annoyed.

"Conner, didn't you hear me call? Lunch has been ready for ten minutes. You've got to show more respect for other people in this house."

"Sorry, Dad. I was doing homework," I said quickly. My eyes flicked to the open closet door. If he stepped into the room and turned, he would see Oscar.

Dad's eyes followed my gaze, and he took a step into the room. My heart pounded with panic, and I leaped up from the bed, hurrying to block his view of the closet.

"I'm starved," I said, trying to distract him. "What are we having?"

Dad grinned and stepped back.

"For someone who's starving," he laughed, "you're sure taking your time getting to the food. But I'm glad you're doing your homework," he added. "You won't achieve anything worthwhile in this life without hard work and commitment."

Give me a break. I wished I could make Dad see that I was willing to commit to things and work hard at them. I just didn't want to commit to piano.

The Truth About Rats

After lunch, I returned to my room with a chunk of cheese and a slice of apple in my pocket. I'd also saved a couple of black beans from the soup Dad had heated up.

"I'll be on the computer," Dad called to me before I shut my bedroom door. That was good. He'd be busy for quite a while, and Jenna had gone over to a friend's house. But I wished my door had a lock on it.

Grabbing the rat book off the bed, I went to kneel on the floor by Oscar's cage. As usual, Oscar stood up to greet me.

"Hey, Oscar," I said, opening the cage roof door. "I've got some treats for you."

I broke off a tiny piece of cheese and reached into the cage with it. Oscar's nose twitched with interest and he stretched up eagerly. He obviously liked the smell of the cheese. I paused before giving it to him, getting a new idea.

What if I laid all the food out for Oscar to choose from? Would he go for the cheese first?

I withdrew my hand and placed the piece of cheese on the floor in front of me. I set one of the black beans and a piece of the apple slice on the floor as well, spacing the three pieces of food evenly. Then I took Oscar out of the cage. I held his warm furry body against my chest for a moment, stroking his fur.

"I've got some food for you, Oscar," I whispered to him. "Let's see which one you like the best."

I set Oscar down on the floor in front of the three pieces of food. He crouched, his nose sniffing the air. I leaned forward . Was he going to go for the cheese? Oscar didn't move. What was he waiting for? He'd seemed eager enough for the cheese when I held it in his cage.

Suddenly Oscar jerked forward, but instead of heading for the food, he made an about-face and scurried between my knees.

"Hey, what are you doing?" I whispered. "The food is over there."

I picked up Oscar and placed him back in front of the food. Again he turned and ran for my knees. What was he up to? I shifted backward, away from him. He moved, as if about to follow my knees. Of course, he was looking for a place to hide. How dumb of me to forget. I leaned forward to pick Oscar up, but at that moment he must have changed his mind about aiming for my knees. Instead he made a dash for my dresser, which stood against the wall near the closet. I reached for him, but not quickly enough. In an instant he had disappeared into the narrow gap under the dresser.

I groaned. How was I going to get him out of there? The bottom of the dresser had a decorative strip of curly-edged wood that blocked off most of the gap. I knew, from trying to dig stray Lego pieces out of there, that it was hard to get my hand in very far.

I lay down on the floor and pressed my cheek against the carpet to try to see Oscar. I could just make out his shape in the shadows at the back of the dresser. Experimentally, I poked my hand in under the middle of the dresser, but I could only reach in as far as my elbow. My fingers brushed against Oscar's fur, but I couldn't get hold of him.

I withdrew my hand and sat up again. I'd had to use a long ruler to pull out the pieces of Lego, but I was sure that wouldn't work with Oscar, and I didn't want to risk hurting or scaring him either.

I glanced at my closed bedroom door, wondering if Dad was about to look in on me again. Beyond the door, the house was quiet.

I looked around me. What should I do? Would Oscar eventually come out if I waited? What if he didn't? My eyes fell on the book lying on my bed. Maybe there'd be something in there that could help.

I retrieved the book from the bed, keeping one eye on the bottom of the dresser the whole time in case Oscar decided to come out. I didn't want to accidentally step on him. But I didn't have to worry about that. He was staying put.

I sat back down on the floor and flipped through the book. I'm not sure what I was looking for—maybe a section called How To Remove a Rat From Under a Dresser. Of course there wasn't one, but something else caught my eye: How To Catch a Rat.

If your rat is loose and you want to get him back in his cage quickly, entice him with food. When the rat comes to check out the treat, pick him up and return him to his cage.

Well, that was easier said than done. Oscar didn't seem interested in food right now, but it was worth a try. I picked up the cheese, bean and apple from the floor and went to the closet to get a few Cheerios and some more cheese, which I knew Oscar liked. I placed the cheese and one Cheerio just outside the opening under the dresser; then I put another small piece of cheese, another Cheerio and the rest of the food a little farther away from the dresser. Still no movement under the dresser.

I sat back with a sigh and opened the book again, holding it so that I could see the pages and the bottom of the dresser at the same time. I guessed I was going to have to wait Oscar out. I riffled through the pages, reading the chapter titles, then stopped when Understanding Your Rat" caught my eye. I began to read.

To understand your pet rat's behavior, you need to know about the habits of its wild ancestors.

By now the image of hoards of filthy, black, yellow-fanged rats swarming over our back steps seemed foolish and cartoony. I realized that since I'd met Oscar, my understanding of rats had really changed. I read further.

Wild rats like to sleep in dark places.

Well that was good. Oscar must like my closet then.

Although they are crepuscular, meaning they can be active or asleep at different times during both day and night, rats usually come out to hunt at dawn or dusk. They are cautious animals who like to hide and are not comfortable in bright light or wide open spaces.

I had learned about that last bit, all right. My bedroom must have looked like a wide open, scary space to Oscar. I should have let him get more comfortable with his new surroundings before letting him out on the floor, and I should have blocked off the places I didn't want him to go.

I set the book aside again and bent down to take another look at Oscar. He was still at the back of the dresser, but now he was sitting on his hind legs, grooming himself. I felt better. Grooming was a good sign, wasn't it? He wouldn't do that if he was still scared, would he? Maybe he'd eat now.

I took one of the cheese pieces in my fingers and held it under the dresser.

"Oscar," I called coaxingly. "I've got some nice cheese for you."

Knock, knock.

I jumped, dropping the cheese.

"Conner," Dad called through the closed door. "Jake is on the phone."

Heart thudding, I silently urged Oscar to stay hidden. But it was okay. Dad didn't come in this time.

"Tell him I'll call him back in a few minutes," I called from my frozen position on the floor. I hadn't even heard the phone ring.

"All right," Dad said, his voice trailing off as he moved away from the door.

I waited a second to make sure he wasn't coming back, then dove forward to peer under the dresser. Oscar was still there, but motionless now. Was he scared again? I lay on the floor watching him. Finally, he resumed grooming, and I sat up to look for the piece of cheese

I'd dropped earlier. It was stuck to my pants.

Taking a deep breath, I returned to the floor and held the cheese out to Oscar for the second time. I waited, my arm extended under the dresser, but nothing happened. After a few more minutes I gave up and pulled my arm back out. Another check under the dresser told me that Oscar was still standing at the back, grooming. At this rate, we'd be here all day. Sighing, I picked up the book once more. Might as well keep reading.

Brown rats live together in packs or family clans. They are social, peaceful animals, and squabbles are rare. Each rat has its own job in the extended family…

There! A flash of movement caught my eye. A grayish brown nose with a pink tip poked out from under the dresser, snatched up the first piece of cheese, then disappeared. Quietly, I closed the book and carefully set it down out of the way.

The nose appeared again, twitching. Cautiously, Oscar crept out toward the next piece of food, and I scooped him up with both hands.

"Maybe we'll stick to the top of the bed for now," I told him.

Jake

On Monday morning I sat down at my desk at school, grinning to myself. I'd progressed a lot with Oscar over the weekend. I'd even gotten him to jump through a hoop for a piece of cheese The hoop was a plastic hair band I'd borrowed from Jenna's room while she was out. It was open at one end, but when I held it upside down it made a good hoop. I turned to Jake, eager to tell him about Oscar, though I wasn't sure if he'd be interested. Jake didn't look at me. Instead he stared straight ahead as if I wasn't there. I nudged his shoulder to get his attention. He jerked away and turned to glare at me.

"What do you want?" he snarled.

My mouth dropped open. What was wrong with him?

"Well?" he asked.

"Nothing," I said. I wasn't about to tell him about Oscar now.

"Good morning, everyone," Miss Chien announced at the front of the room, drawing my attention away from Jake.

Math period dragged on. By recess I still didn't know what was eating Jake. I tried to stick with him as everyone moved outside, but Mercedes and Erika headed me off.

"How's Oscar?" Mercedes asked, her red coat like a big stop sign. Erika pushed up beside her, anxious to hear what I had to say.

For a second I felt torn, wanting to talk to them about the animals, but also wanting to go after Jake. He looked back over his shoulder once, scowled and jogged away toward the soccer field. I shrugged and turned back to Mercedes and Erika.

"Oscar's great," I told them. "How about your rats?" I asked Erika.

"They're okay. I think the dogs scared them at first, but the rats are already ignoring them. Anyway, they stay in their cage unless the dogs are out of the house or the rats are locked safely in my bedroom."

"But do they get exercise every day?" Mercedes asked.

"Yeah, I make sure they have some time to run around when it's safe," Erika said.

"What about your hamster?" I asked Mercedes.

"You mean Missy?" she corrected. She waved her hands dramatically. "Oh, she gets plenty of exercise, all right. She keeps me awake all night running on her squeaky wheel."

We were laughing as Annie ran up, out of breath.

"You won't believe what my rabbit did yesterday," she said, grabbing hold of Mercedes.

"What?" All eyes turned to her.

"She jumped up on the couch and peed, she chewed through the cord to the TV..."

Erika and Mercedes exclaimed sympathetically and laughed at the same time as Annie's list continued.

"But she's cute, right?" Mercedes said.

"Not as cute as I thought when I agreed to foster her," Annie complained.

"Don't worry," said Erika. "You only have two weeks to go."

Only two weeks. Two weeks of keeping Oscar hidden. Could I do it? And what about after that?

"I'll see you guys later," I told them suddenly. "I'm supposed to be playing soccer."

I jogged away to find Jake. I wasn't sure what kind of reception he'd give me on the soccer field, but I didn't want to think about the end of the two weeks.

"Which side should I go on?" I called to the boy standing between the closest goal posts.

"Ours," he called back. "We're short one."

I ran onto the field, looking around to try to get a sense of who was on which team. The ball was heading toward me down the field with Jake running after it. I hurried to intercept, but he beat me to it. Instead of sending the ball toward the goal, he kicked it straight for my head. It came at me like a bullet, and I instinctively jumped out of the way. There was no way I was going to try heading it.

"Watch it!" I yelled. What had he done that for?

"Sorry. Didn't see you," Jake said with a sneer. "I thought you were off playing with your girlfriends."

Anger boiled up in me.

"What's wrong with you?" I demanded, giving Jake a shove. He'd obviously kicked the ball at me on purpose.

"What's wrong with *you*?" Jake snapped, shoving me back.

"Hey, are you guys playing or what?" someone called as the ball rolled by and neither Jake nor I went for it.

We continued to glare at each other, and before either of us could decide what his next move should be, the bell rang to end recess. Without another word, Jake pushed past me, heading back to the school. For a second I stood watching him. This was stupid. We were supposed to be friends.

Quickly, I caught up to Jake and grabbed his shoulder. He jerked away, scowling.

"What are you so mad about?" I demanded.

Jake continued walking, but I kept up with him. I didn't think he was going to answer me. Then he stopped and turned to face me.

"I thought we were best friends," he said, his face a mask. "But you spend all your time with that stupid animal club and those girls."

I started to protest, but Jake continued.

"We were supposed to take our bikes to the skateboard park on Saturday," he said accusingly.

Suddenly I remembered. The phone call. Jake had called me when Oscar was stuck under the dresser, and I'd forgotten to phone him back. I hadn't even thought about Jake the whole weekend.

"I know, I know," I said. "I'm sorry I forgot to call you, but something came up."

"Yeah, sure," he grumbled sarcastically. He started to walk away.

I hesitated a second, then made a quick decision.

"Wait!" I called after Jake. "Do you like rats?"

Rat Problem

There was an unfamiliar white truck parked in the driveway when Jake and I rode our bikes up to my house after school.

At first, when I'd tried to tell Jake about Oscar, he hadn't wanted to listen. But then he got interested, despite being mad at me.

"You're kidding? You're hiding a rat in your room?" Jake had exclaimed, sounding impressed.

When I'd invited him to come over and meet Oscar, he'd agreed right away. By the time we got to my house, our confrontation on the soccer field had been forgotten.

We stopped to look at the truck. A dark blue logo on the door had a picture of a raccoon and the words *Wildlife Control*. Jake and I looked at each other. Wildlife control? What was that doing at my house? Anxiety sprouted in my chest.

"Come on," I said, pointing my bike toward the back of the house. My mind leapt in wild directions. Were the animal control people here for the rat in the backyard? Or were they here for Oscar?

The back gate was open. I jumped off my bike and pushed it through, not knowing what to expect. Inside the yard I halted suddenly, and Jake's front wheel bumped into my leg. Mom was standing by the back steps talking to an ordinary-looking man with short dark hair, jeans and a dark blue bomber jacket. There was a small design on the chest of his jacket that matched the logo on the truck door.

"If rats are in your yard, they could be in your home as well," the man was saying.

I met Jake's eyes, and I could tell he knew exactly what I was thinking. Oscar. At least it sounded like the man hadn't been in the house yet.

"Conner, you're home," Mom said, catching sight of Jake and me. "Hello, Jake."

She looked a bit embarrassed—like when unexpected guests catch her with a messy kitchen or using a cake mix.

"This is Mr. Merchanko," she said, gesturing toward the man. "He's come to look at our… ah…rat problem."

"We've only seen signs of the one out here," I said quickly.

"Well, if you've only got one, you're lucky," the man said. "If there's only one, we might be able to trap it. But usually where there's one, there's several more, and there's no point in putting out traps. You might catch the first one, but the others will get wise pretty fast. Rats are smart. They learn quickly to avoid traps."

"But then what can we do?" Mom asked.

The man took a few steps around the garbage can area, looking it over before answering.

"Rats have a relatively small territory around their food source," the man said. He nodded at the garbage can. "Best thing you can do is block off their food source, and they'll look for a new one somewhere else."

"How do we do that?" Mom asked.

"Make sure they can't get into that garbage can," he said. He pointed to the bottom of the can. "You've got a hole there that's like a welcome sign to rats. I suggest you replace that can with one rats can't chew through. And…"

He looked around the yard, considering. I waited for what he would say next, my hands sweating.

He pointed to the right of the garbage can.

"I suggest you remove those bushes," he said. "Rats don't like open spaces, and those bushes provide perfect cover for them to get in close."

I decided the man knew what he was talking about. What he was saying about the wild rat matched perfectly with what I had discovered about Oscar.

"Do you have any pets?" the man asked Mom. My heart jumped at the unexpectedness of the question, and I glanced at Jake, who raised an eyebrow at me.

"No," Mom said quickly. "Why do you ask?"

"I was just wondering if you leave any pet food outside," the man explained. "Any food left outside will attract rats. You want to get rid of any food source around your house. You might want to talk to your neighbors as well. Bird seed, compost, pet food left out on a porch, fruit trees where the fruit has fallen on the ground—those are all things that can attract rats and keep them coming around."

Mom nodded grimly, but she looked hopeful—like the suggestions were something she could handle.

"All right," she said. "That sounds reasonable."

"Can't you put out poison for the rats?" Jake asked.

I gave him a sharp look. I didn't want poison around our house. But I didn't have to worry.

"We don't use poison," the man said. "Rats can eat it and die in the walls of your house."

Mom made a face at that.

"What about cats and other animals that come around? They could eat the poison too," I pointed out.

"That's right," the man agreed. "Sometimes other animals get caught in traps too."

"All right," Mom said briskly, sounding like she'd had enough talk about rats and animals getting caught in traps and poisoned around her house. "So we'll work on the garbage issue, clear out the shrubs and talk to the neighbors."

As she spoke, she began ushering Mr. Merchanko back toward the gate, seeming in a hurry to have him leave now. Jake and I set our bikes aside and started up the stairs to the house.

"That wasn't so bad," Jake whispered.

"Yeah," I said. "No thanks to you. You sounded like you wanted the guy to put poison out."

Jake tilted his head to show he was considering this.

"It would have been interesting," he said.

Disgusted, I gave him a shove. He pretended he was losing his balance and about to fall down the stairs. Then he steadied himself and laughed.

"Just kidding," he said.

I turned my back on Jake and pushed open the kitchen door, trying not to let him see me smile. Sometimes I didn't know what to make of Jake, but he did know how to make me laugh, even when I didn't want to.

In the kitchen Jake wanted to stop for a snack, but I was anxious to check on Oscar first. All the talk about getting rid of rats made me nervous.

"Hurry," I told Jake as I pulled him into my bedroom and closed the door behind us.

Jake looked around the room.

"Where is it?" he asked.

"*It* is a *he*, and his name is Oscar," I said, moving to the closet. I swung open the door, and Jake came up behind me.

"Cool," he said as he caught sight of Oscar, who sat on his hind legs and stared up at us from the middle of his cage.

Once again I felt a wash of relief as I knelt down to open the cage and lift Oscar out. He sat in my arms and smelled me as I straightened up; then he climbed up to my shoulder and snuggled up beside my neck where he could get a good view of Jake, the stranger, and still feel safe. His tiny claws pricked through the fabric of my shirt as he held on.

"Did you teach him to do that?" Jake asked, looking at Oscar with interest.

"No, he does it on his own," I admitted. "But I'll show you something I did teach him."

I got out a handful of dried food and Jenna's hair band, then took Oscar over to the bed. First I made a tunnel with folds of the duvet cover so Oscar would have a place to hide.

"Watch this," I said.

I set Oscar down on the bed, and he ran straight for the tunnel. Jake laughed. I waited until Oscar felt comfortable enough to poke his nose out of his hiding spot (it didn't take very long anymore), then I held out a piece of cereal with the hair band between the food and Oscar. Oscar sniffed the air for a moment, then crept out from the tunnel. He stood on his back legs, his nose twitching.

Then he leapt through the hair band and snatched up the cereal.

"Cool!" Jake exclaimed again.

I set the hair band aside and let Oscar run back to his hiding spot to eat.

"Do you think he'd do it for me?" Jake asked.

"Maybe you should let him smell you first, so he gets used to you," I suggested.

I peeked into the tunnel. Oscar had finished eating, so I picked him up with both hands and held him out to Jake. For a second Jake looked uncertain, and I thought he might pull away, but then he opened his hands and I placed Oscar into them.

Jake stared at Oscar for a moment, looking incredulous—like he couldn't believe he was standing there holding a rat.

"I can feel his claws," Jake said, amazed.

Jake shifted Oscar's body to one hand and supported him against his chest. Then, with his other hand, he tentatively reached a finger out to pet Oscar's head.

"Wow, this is so weird." Jake grinned.

I laughed. I could hardly believe it myself. Jake was doing animal stuff with me. Jake was petting my rat.

"I mean," Jake continued, "it's weird to have that guy outside trying to get rid of rats when you've got one right here."

"Yeah," I agreed, no longer laughing. Pests or pets? I was sure the rest of my family would only see it one way.

Caught

On Tuesday after school, Jake came over to visit Oscar again, and we managed to get in some bike practice. On Wednesday, I was surprised that Jake wanted to come with me to the animal club meeting. He even helped clean Daisy's cage, though he joked around and made stupid comments—like pretending something was wrong with Daisy when he couldn't find her tail. I saw the girls exchange looks more than once, as if they weren't sure they wanted him there. Sean was at the meeting too, so there was an even number of boys and girls for a change.

"I wish I hadn't been sick when you went on the shelter visits," Sean said as he dumped new shavings into Daisy's enclosure.

"We can go there again," Erika said. "I think they'd like us to come every week if we can."

"I should be able to make it this Friday," Sean said. "Are you coming too?" he asked Jake.

Jake hesitated.

"Maybe," he answered.

Surprised, I looked at Jake. He shrugged.

"I wouldn't mind seeing the other rats," he said.

This started a discussion of which small animals we liked the best and which ones we thought would make the best pets. After hearing about the latest destructive exploits of Annie's rabbit and the continued midnight squeaking of Mercedes' athletic hamster, we all agreed that we preferred guinea pigs and rats.

Our meeting finished shortly after four, and I rode my bike home from school in a good mood. I could hardly believe that Jake was becoming interested in the animal club.

When I arrived home, I knew right away that something was wrong. Mom was standing in the living room window, watching for me. As soon as she caught sight of me, she moved away from the window. Dread knifed through my body.

I pushed my bike through the gate at the side of the house and over to the back door of the garage, my hands starting to feel clammy. This was it. She'd found Oscar. What had she done with him? I tried to tell myself that she could be upset about something else. Maybe someone was sick. Maybe something had happened to Yeh Yeh or Ma Ma.

After shutting my bike away, I started up the back steps, my legs like lead. Before I had reached the top step, the back door opened and Mom stood there, her face grim and her arms crossed over her chest. Whatever it was, it wasn't good.

"It's about time you got home," Mom said coldly. "You have some explaining to do."

So it wasn't Yeh Yeh or Ma Ma. That was good at least. But I didn't like what that left. I looked down, avoiding meeting Mom's eyes as she stepped aside to let me through the door.

"I vacuumed in your bedroom this morning," Mom went on. She didn't have to say more.

Oscar!

Mom saw the panic that leapt into my face.

"Don't worry," she said coldly, her arms still crossed tightly over her chest. "I didn't touch the dirty thing. It's in your closet where I found it."

She paused as if waiting for me to say something, but before I could start to explain, words burst out of Mom like rain from a storm cloud.

"I can't believe you would do this. A rat, of all things. You know how we feel about pets. And behind our backs…"

Her arms uncrossed and she grabbed hold of my shoulders, steering me down the hall to my bedroom as she continued her tirade. She stopped at the doorway and pointed a shaking finger in the direction of my closet. "I want that rat out of this house now!"

"Okay, okay," I said quickly, going to the closet.

What was I going to do? My mind whirled. I'd have to take Oscar back to the shelter. What would Mini say when she found out I'd misled her about having permission to take him? What would the others say? Would someone else take Oscar? Would I ever see him again?

I looked down at Oscar, who stood in his cage peering up at me, expectant and trusting. I took a deep breath and turned back to Mom. I'd have to at least try to explain.

"I didn't mean to bring him in the house behind your back," I said. "It just happened."

Mom stood in the doorway, her arms crossed again, her lips a thin angry line.

"You'll have to do better than that," she said.

"I'm just taking care of him," I continued. "To help the animal shelter."

"The animal shelter?" Mom said, a note of incredulity in her voice. "I can't believe they would let a child have an animal without the parents' permission."

"I guess they thought I had your permission," I admitted.

"You lied to them?" Mom's anger flared up again.

"No," I said quickly. "I didn't say I had your permission. I just didn't say I didn't."

"A lie by omission," Mom pointed out sternly, though I thought I caught a twitch at one corner of her mouth.

"And did you say you could keep this rat?" Mom asked.

"No," I explained. "I only said I could take care of him—Oscar—for two weeks or so."

"Oscar?" she asked. Was there a touch of amusement in her voice?

"Yes, that's his name. I could show him to you," I added tentatively.

This time Mom did smile—a small tight smile that did not quite make it to her eyes.

"I'm not sure if I'm ready to be on a first-name basis," she said, holding up her palms to ward us off.

"I'll just bring his cage over," I said.

When she didn't object, I lifted up Oscar's cage and brought it over to my bed where she could see him better.

"He's really not that bad," I said. "He's not dirty at all."

Mom looked Oscar over without moving any closer.

"That may be," she said. "But he's still a rat. And you had no right to bring him into this house." Her arms crossed again. "You'll have to take him back."

I looked at my watch. It was almost five. A spark of hope flared inside me.

"The shelter closes at five," I said. "We wouldn't be able to get there in time, and they're not expecting us."

Mom frowned. "He'll have to go back first thing tomorrow, then. And you're going to have to explain this to your father as soon as he's home."

"I know," I said, a fresh wave of dread splashing up inside me. At the same time, though, I was relieved. It was all out in the open. The stress and worry of hiding Oscar was over. I didn't have to lie anymore. But now I was going to have to give him up.

Jenna Surprises

I was practicing the piano when Dad got home. I heard him talking to Mom in the kitchen. Was she telling him about Oscar? My fingers stumbled through the minuet. I was supposed to have it memorized by now, and my fingers did manage to keep going while my ears tried to hear what Mom and Dad were saying in the next room. But when I hit a wrong note, I became conscious of playing the piano again, and my fingers came to a faltering stop. I had no idea where I was in the piece. I looked up at my music book, found a spot in the middle of the minuet and placed my fingers over the keys again.

Plunk, plunk. It was hopeless. I couldn't concentrate, and my fingers wouldn't get going again. I leaned forward and closed up the music book. Maybe Mom and Dad wouldn't notice if I finished a little early today.

When I got up from the piano bench and turned around, Dad was waiting for me.

"Mom says you have something to tell me," he said. From the steely tone of his voice and the grim set to his face, I gathered he must already have an idea of what I'd done. Was hiding a rat in my room really so bad?

Dad ushered me down the hall to my bedroom, where Oscar waited in his cage on my bed. He ignored the cage and waited for me to explain.

"What bothers us the most, Conner," Dad began when I'd finished explaining, "is that you went behind our backs. You did something you knew we wouldn't have given permission for."

"I know," I said, looking down at the floor. "I shouldn't have done it, but the others were all allowed…" I knew this wasn't the right thing to say. I could hear Dad's intake of breath as he got ready to give the *If your friends jumped off a cliff, would you do that too?* lecture.

"And I really wanted to help the animals," I added.

Dad paused.

"I understand that you wanted to help," he said carefully. "That's admirable. But you can't do it by lying or misleading people or by disobeying the rules of this house and showing disrespect to your parents."

He was really laying on the guilt, and it was working. I wanted to sink into the floor.

"I'm really sorry, Dad," I said, wondering if my parents would ever trust me again.

I looked down at Oscar and unconsciously reached my finger through the bars on top his cage. Oscar stretched up and sniffed my finger, tickling me with his whiskers. It was what he did every time, but it felt like he was trying to offer me some comfort.

"How long did you tell the shelter you were going to look after him?" Dad asked, the hard edge to his voice softening slightly.

"Two weeks or so."

"And how many days have you had him now?"

"Five days, including today," I answered. I raised my eyes to meet Dad's, a tiny spark of hope lighting in my chest.

"That's less than a week and a half to go," I pointed out. I took a deep breath. If there was a chance of persuading Dad I should finish looking after Oscar, I had to go for it.

"You always say we need to follow through with our commitments," I pointed out.

Dad's eyes narrowed, his thick eyebrows becoming a dark V above them.

"Yes, I do say that, don't I?" he said. "But it's a bit different when you committed to something you weren't allowed to commit to in the first place."

"I know," I said, looking down again.

Dad sighed.

"Well," he said. "I'll talk to your mother about it, but before I do that, you'd better show me how you've been taking care of this rat without anyone knowing he was here."

I looked up at Dad and grinned.

After Dad left my room, there was a knock on my door. Jenna stepped in without waiting for an invitation.

"Hey!" I started to protest.

"I can't believe you've been hiding a rat in here!" she said, ignoring me and looking around.

Oscar was sitting on my shoulder, and I held on to him protectively, not sure what Jenna would do when she saw him. She spied him at once.

"Oh, he's so cute," she said. "Can I touch him?"

"Sure," I said, surprised. I guess I'd been expecting her to say something insulting or to at least act creeped out.

She reached out her hand.

"Let him sniff you first," I suggested.

She pulled her hand back quickly.

"Does he bite?" she asked, alarmed.

"No," I laughed. "I just didn't want you to scare him."

"Oh."

Her hand went out again, and this time she held it up to Oscar's nose.

"His whiskers are so funny," she whispered.

"Do you want to hold him?" I asked. Trying to see what was happening on my shoulder made my neck sore.

"Can I?" she asked.

I hesitated a few seconds. This was my annoying sister Jenna, after all. I wasn't sure if I wanted her getting close to Oscar. But it was hard to ignore her interest, and I guess I was kind of pleased to be able to show Oscar off a bit.

I lifted him from my shoulder and put him in Jenna's arms.

"You can sit on the bed if you want," I suggested.

"Thanks."

She sat down, cradling Oscar in her arms as if he were a doll or a baby.

"What does he eat?" she asked.

I sat down beside Jenna and began to tell her all about Oscar. It was weird having her ask me questions and knowing more than she did about something for a change.

"Hey, what's my hair band doing in here?" she asked suddenly, jumping to her feet.

I caught sight of the red hair band sitting on my dresser. Oops. I was glad Oscar was still in Jenna's hands. She remembered him and sat down again, moving more carefully.

"Ah…I borrowed it," I tried to explain.

"You *borrowed* it." She gave me a disbelieving look, eyes narrowed. "Since when do you wear girls' hair stuff? And what were you doing in my room without my permission?" she demanded.

"I'll show you," I told her. I took the hair band off the dresser and got a couple of pieces of food out of Oscar's food container.

"Let me have Oscar back for a minute," I said.

Jenna handed him over, then crossed her arms over her chest and frowned, looking just like Mom had earlier.

I placed Oscar on the bed and held the band in front of him, my fingers closing off the open part.

"Jump, Oscar," I commanded.

Oscar jumped through the hoop, and Jenna clapped her hands in delight, her angry look evaporating.

"Suppertime." Mom's voice interrupted us.

Jenna and I looked up, startled. Mom was standing in the hall, watching us. How long had she been there? Had she seen Oscar do his trick?

"It's good to see the two of you getting along for a change," Mom commented, looking from me to Jenna. But she didn't say anything about Oscar—just turned and walked back to the kitchen.

"I hope you get to keep him," Jenna whispered as I put Oscar back in his cage.

Verdict

Mom and Dad looked at me across the kitchen table, their faces serious. The food lay in front of us, untouched. I sat frozen in my chair like an accused criminal waiting for the judges to give their verdict.

"We're not happy about your behavior," Dad began. Mom's lips remained a tight line as she nodded in agreement.

"But the animal shelter shouldn't suffer for your mistake," Dad continued. "We've decided that you should follow through on your commitment to look after the rat for two weeks."

My heart leapt. I couldn't believe it. I heard Jenna's hands come together in an involuntary clap of excitement, and I was grateful that she was on my side for a change.

"But we better not ever see that rodent out of your room," Mom added firmly.

I nodded.

"And there's going to be a punishment," Dad went on.

"Your mother and I are not happy with how you went about things."

I nodded again.

"We've decided to ground you for the next two weekends," Mom concluded. "No meeting up with Jake. No bike riding."

"You can stay home and help around the house," Dad added.

"But what about piano?" I asked. No bike for two whole weekends would be hard, but if being grounded meant I didn't have to go to piano lessons, it wouldn't be a punishment at all.

"Piano lessons are still on," Dad said, a little annoyed. "You can ride your bike to your lesson and then straight back home."

I sighed. "Okay."

"All right then," Dad said, taking up his fork. "I think we understand each other." He looked at Mom for confirmation, and she gave him a nod and a half smile.

"Now, let's eat," she said, "before this food gets any colder."

I tried to look contrite as I dug into my food, but inside I was cheering. I could keep Oscar—at least for a little longer.

Under the table, I felt Jenna's foot give me a nudge. I looked up, expecting to see her gloat over my grounding. But instead she gave me a quick smile. She liked Oscar too.

After supper I returned to my room. Oscar's cage was still on my bed in full view of the open door. I could set it anywhere I wanted now. Looking around, I decided on a spot under the window. I moved the cage to its new location, then bent down to take Oscar out. I could hardly believe my luck. I was allowed to take care of Oscar. I pushed away all thoughts of what was going to happen at the end of the two weeks.

The next day, Jake came over after school again. We visited with Oscar for a while, then went outside to do some bike practice before it got dark. It was such a relief to be able to leave Oscar for whole chunks of time without worrying about him being discovered.

There was never much traffic on the road in front of our house, so we took our bikes out there. I started with a few bunny hops, jumping the bike up and down, using my body to lift it up off the ground. It was one of the first tricks I'd learned. Once you knew how to do it, it was pretty easy, and it was fun to see how much lift you could get. Jake attempted to lift his front tire off the ground and do a wheelie, but when he didn't have much success he shifted to a rear peg manual, standing on the back pegs of his bike and swinging one leg to keep the bike going.

"Not bad," I called after him. "But we should work on the combos we're going to do for the competition."

For mine, I thought I'd start with a hop 180, then do a roll back and a bar spin. Working on the 180, I hopped the bike up, then turned the handlebars and my body hard to the right, trying to get the bike to rotate while it was still in the air. Remember to look at the spot where you want to land, I told myself. On the first try I made about a quarter turn. Finally, after several attempts, I did a 180 in midair before the tires clunked down to the ground.

"Hey, that's pretty good," Jake commented as he bailed on the trick he was working on and jumped clear of his bike.

"Not quite there," I said, getting ready to try again.

"I can't get the bar hop right," Jake complained. "Can you show me how to do it again?"

I steadied my bike, locked my elbows in place on the handlebars and tucked my knees to my chest, bringing my feet over the handlebars, then dropping them to my front pegs. I balanced on the front pegs for several seconds, then reversed back over the handlebars, one leg at a time.

Gritting his teeth in concentration, Jake attempted to copy me. He gripped the handlebars, lifted his knees and caught his feet on the handlebars. The bike wobbled, and he jumped free.

"Just practice clearing the bars first," I suggested, "without trying to land on the pegs."

I turned back to my own bike.

"Car!" Jake called.

I turned to see Dad's car approaching slowly. He was home already. Was it that late? I hadn't practiced the piano yet.

"I've gotta go in!" I told Jake, turning my bike toward the house.

"All right," Jake said reluctantly. "I guess I better get going then."

But before Jake could take off, the car pulled into our driveway and stopped beside us, continuing to idle. Dad rolled down the window.

"It looks like you boys are getting pretty good at some of those stunts," he called out.

"Conner is at least," Jake said, smiling at Dad. "See you, Mr. Lee," he added with a wave as he pedaled away.

Dad turned to me, his eyes narrowing.

"I'll talk to you as soon as I park the car," he said.

I nodded and headed for the back gate while Dad put the car in the garage. We met at the bottom of the back steps.

"You were looking good out there," Dad said, stuffing his keys into his jacket pocket and adjusting his briefcase under his other arm. "But I thought you were supposed to be grounded."

"Just the weekends," I pointed out. He'd said I was looking good. But what could he have seen from the car? Did he really mean it?

"Just weekends?" Dad repeated. "Sounds like a bit of an oversight."

Panic snuffed out the good feeling I'd had at Dad's earlier words. He wasn't going to ground me for the weekdays too, was he? How would I get ready for the bike competition? I had to tell him.

"Dad," I began, my mouth dry. "I'm not just doing bike tricks for fun, I'm practicing for a competition."

He paused at the top of the stairs and looked at me. "What kind of competition?"

"Flatland," I said, then explained that this meant I had to put together a combination of tricks to perform on a flat surface—in this case, the community center parking lot.

Dad gave me an appraising look.

"I didn't know the bike stuff was so serious," he said. "You can keep working at it—as long as it doesn't interfere with homework or piano practice," he added pointedly.

"Thanks, Dad," I said, relieved.

He opened the back door and paused, looking meaningfully at his watch.

"I'll get to the piano right away," I said quickly, ducking past him and into the kitchen. My heart pounded. I had to show Dad and Mom that I could handle it all—piano, school, bike practice and looking after Oscar. But could I?

Expectations

"Sunday is Chinese New Year," Mom reminded us at supper. "We're going to have our family dinner at Ma Ma and Yeh Yeh's on Friday night."

In school that morning, Miss Chien had talked about Chinese New Year and how it follows a lunar calendar, beginning on the second new moon after the winter solstice. Winter solstice is like a turning point in the year. The daylight hours start getting longer again after that.

Miss Chien said that lots of cultures around the world have celebrations of light at this time of year. There's Christmas, Hanukah, Diwali, Chinese New Year and lots of others. People used to believe that rituals actually helped spring arrive. If we were really traditional Chinese, we would have our dinner on New Year's Eve, but we just try for a night relatively close to it, when everyone can be there.

"I'm going to make some *gok jai* to bring to the dinner," Mom was saying. *Gok jai* are crescent-shaped Chinese cookies with sweet filling inside—one of my favorites.

"Jenna's going to help me," she added, smiling at Jenna, who smiled sweetly in return.

I squirmed in my chair. There was Jenna, kissing up to Mom again.

"Just as long as you don't bring flowers to the dinner," Dad said to Mom with a chuckle.

I had to laugh. It was a private family joke that had to do with something that happened when Dad and Mom were first married. Back then, Mom had tried to please her new mother-in-law by bringing her a bouquet of white roses, but it had the opposite effect. Ma Ma got upset, and Mom couldn't figure out why. Dad wasn't sure either—I guess because he hadn't realized that Ma Ma never had white flowers in the house. Apparently, in traditional Chinese culture, white flowers are only for funerals. Ma Ma had complained to Yeh Yeh in Cantonese that Dad's new wife wanted her dead before her time, and Dad had caught enough of it to figure out what was going on. After that, Mom decided it was safer to stay away from flowers altogether.

"I don't think she'll be able to find anything wrong with cookies," Mom said, looking annoyed.

"You really don't need to bring anything," Dad said.

"But she never lets me help," Mom complained.

For the first time it occurred to me that maybe Mom felt

bad that Ma Ma always cooked the big Chinese New Year dinner and never asked Mom to help. Mom was a professional cook, after all. Didn't Ma Ma think she could cook well enough? Or was it because Mom wasn't Chinese?

"I'm looking forward to that piano recital," Dad said, changing the subject.

Suddenly my food got difficult to chew.

Jenna brightened.

"I'm going to be playing the Minute Waltz by Chopin and Bach's Prelude and Fugue in C minor," she said enthusiastically.

"That sounds lovely," Mom said, looking cheerful again.

"What about you, Conner?" Dad asked.

I swallowed hard, afraid the lump of food would get stuck in my throat.

"Well?" Dad prompted.

I gestured at my throat and reached for my milk glass.

"He's supposed to play a Mozart minuet," Jenna answered for me.

I glared at her. She could have let me answer—instead of having to sound so on top of everything.

"I'm sure it will be very nice," Mom said, giving me an encouraging smile.

Not likely, I wanted to say, but I bit back the words. Mom and Dad looked at me, their eyes full of hope, like they really did expect that, with a bit more practice, I'd be as good as Jenna. How could I tell them that I was going to disappoint them again? Across from me sat Jenna, looking happy and confident. Her long slim fingers rested on the table as if on piano keys. Playing piano was part of who she was. It wasn't part of me. Would Mom and Dad ever see that?

After supper, I retreated to my room and Oscar's company. At least *he* seemed to like me for who I was.

Chinese New Year

"*Gung Hay Fat Choy*!" Jenna and I greeted Ma Ma as she opened the door.

Ma Ma was wearing a red Chinese-style dress, and her round face crinkled into a wide smile at our words. The Chinese New Year's greeting was one of the few bits of Cantonese Jenna and I knew.

"*Sun Nien Fai Lok*!" Ma Ma replied. "*Gung Hay Fat Choy*."

Jenna handed Ma Ma the plate of cookies covered with plastic wrap.

"They're *gok jai*," Jenna said proudly. "Mom and I made them."

"*Doi jeh*. Thank you," Ma Ma said as she took them. She smiled at Jenna, but she looked past Jenna to Mom and narrowed her eyes slightly, as if to let Mom know she shouldn't have brought anything.

I glanced back at Mom, remembering what she'd said about Ma Ma not finding anything wrong with the cookies. Apparently she had found something wrong—

or maybe it was something wrong with Mom.

"You always do so much work with the food," Mom was saying. "We had to bring something."

As we stepped into the house and slipped off our shoes, I glanced from Mom to Ma Ma. I'd never thought about it before, but there were so many little things Mom did to try to please Ma Ma, following as many Chinese traditions as she could, like buying us new clothes for the New Year and making Chinese cookies. Maybe she was still trying to make up for the white flower mistake—still trying to prove herself to her mother-in-law. Trying to be the kind of daughter-in-law she thought Ma Ma wanted her to be. I felt a wave of sympathy for Mom. Living up to what other people expected of you was hard, no matter how old you were.

My moment of contemplation passed as Ma Ma ushered us into the living room, and we were greeted by a barrage of aunts, uncles and cousins rushing up to say hello. My cousin Ryan hung back at the edge of the room, waiting to catch my eye, and I slipped out of the crowd to talk to him.

At the dinner table, Ryan and I managed to sit beside each other. My mouth watered at the smells wafting off the dishes on the table, and Ma Ma and the aunts kept bringing out more and more platters!

"Mmm, hair. My favorite," Ryan said under his breath as Ma Ma set out a plate of long thin black strands of what I thought was a kind of mushroom or maybe moss.

I stifled a laugh. Ryan was always making comments like that. But the stuff really did look like a plate of hair.

We waited for Yeh Yeh to say it was time to eat, then everyone began reaching for the food. I ignored the hair and helped myself to some fish, which was the food closest to me. I was careful to ignore the head and the tail and take a serving from somewhere in the middle. At home we used plates to eat from, but at Ma Ma's we always used Chinese bowls. I plunked the portion of fish on top of the rice already in my bowl, then picked up my chopsticks. Everyone at the table had chopsticks to eat with, except Ryan's little sister, who was only four. She had enough trouble handling a fork—let alone two sticks.

"Did you see the lovely plant Joe and Diane gave me?" Ma Ma said from her seat at the end of the table opposite Yeh Yeh.

Everyone turned to where Ma Ma was pointing. On top of a low cabinet, Ma Ma had set out Mom and Jenna's cookies and a bowl of mandarin oranges. Beside these stood a large green potted plant that had what looked like miniature oranges growing on it.

I glanced over at Mom. Did she feel slighted because Ma Ma hadn't said anything about the cookies.

"The little oranges symbolize our wish for your prosperity in the new year," Uncle Joe explained, smiling at Ma Ma.

Ryan whispered something about his dad sucking up to Ma Ma.

"The color orange is like gold," Uncle Joe went on. "Gold equals wealth. Everything we do for Chinese New Year has a meaning. Before New Year's Eve, we sweep away the old year and the old problems."

"I didn't see him do any sweeping," Aunty Diane complained in a low voice, getting a laugh from Mom.

"And we welcome in the new year and new luck," Uncle Joe continued, ignoring Aunty. "We eat foods of good fortune."

He pointed to the plate of fish.

"A whole fish, with a head and tail, for a good start and a good finish to the new year."

Ma Ma was beaming and nodding. Yeh Yeh had his gray head bowed over his bowl as he continued to eat, but he kept an amused eye on Uncle Joe. Ryan and I exchanged a look and followed Yeh Yeh's example. Out of the corner of one eye, I watched Uncle Joe pull a plate of green beans closer and pick up the serving spoon, waving it over the beans to emphasize his next words.

"Long beans for long life," he said, scooping up a spoonful of beans and dropping them into his bowl.

"Oh come on," Aunty Diane cut in. "Stop showing off. You just looked all that stuff up on the Internet last night."

Everyone laughed, including Uncle Joe.

"Hey, what can I say?" Uncle Joe said, throwing up his hands. "You look Chinese, people expect you to know about everything Chinese."

"Yeah," I said to Ryan under my breath. "Or they expect you to be good at school and music."

"Or kung fu," Ryan added, holding his hands up in a martial arts pose and making chopping motions.

My dad heard Ryan's comment and smiled, nodding his head.

"It's not that bad nowadays," Dad said. "People are used to different cultures, but when I was a boy there were only a couple of Asian kids in the school. If the other kids thought I knew kung fu, I let them think it. Kept me from getting beat up a few times."

Aunty Diane and Mom exchanged a look.

"You'll never guess what I found in Conner's bedroom the other day," Mom said, obviously trying to change the subject.

I groaned, and Ryan leaned forward, eager to get some dirt on me.

Mom told the story of how she found Oscar while doing her New Year's cleaning. I sank down in my chair.

Aunty Diane gave a shiver.

"I hate rats," she said.

"But Oscar's really cute," Jenna cut in.

"We had a rat in my class at school last year," Ryan said. "He was cool."

I sat up a little straighter, surprised to hear my sister and cousin coming to the defense of rats.

"Rats make good pets," I said, forcing myself to speak up. "But they don't live very long."

"Thank God for that!" Aunty Diane exclaimed.

"There are probably more rats than people here in the city," Uncle Joe chimed in.

"Enough about rats," Ma Ma ordered. "Have some more *fat choy.*"

She held up the dish of hair. Ryan and I looked at each other and couldn't help laughing.

"I was born in the Year of the Rat," Yeh Yeh said quietly. "A good year."

"That's why he's so hard-working and charming," Ma Ma said, with a wink at the rest of us that Yeh Yeh didn't see.

After we finished dinner and the table was cleared, everyone moved to the living room. Ryan and I raced for one of the two couches, then sank down and leaned back, feeling stuffed.

"Bring on the *lai see*," Ryan whispered.

I laughed. *Lai see* are the red envelopes filled with lucky money that the adults give out every New Year. It is definitely a major thing the kids in our family look forward to.

Pretty soon Ma Ma and Aunty Diane began handing out red envelopes.

"Now you wait until New Year's Day to open those," Ma Ma told us.

Ryan and I nodded obediently, but as soon as her back was turned we looked at each other. Our families didn't follow very many traditions. It wasn't even actual New Year's Eve. So why stick to the rules? Without a word we tore open the tops of our envelopes. I felt that familiar little rush of anticipation, even though Ma Ma and Aunty Diane always gave the same amount of money every time.

It would have been a perfect evening if Ma Ma hadn't asked Jenna to play the piano. As the first notes filled the room, a feeling of dread coiled around me like a thick rope. The adult relatives made small sounds of appreciation as Jenna played. The rope tightened around my gut.

"Come on!" I whispered to Ryan, tugging on his sleeve. "Let's get out of here before someone asks me to play."

I Hate Piano!

When we got home from Ma Ma and Yeh Yeh's, I went straight to my room to check on Oscar.

"Hey, buddy," I whispered, reaching one hand in for him to sniff. When he touched his nose to my fingertips, it felt like he was saying hello back.

I picked Oscar up and placed him on top of my bed, then leaned over on my elbows so that my upper body made a shelter. Oscar scurried under me, and I ducked my head to look in at him. He stood on his hind legs and touched my nose with his.

After a while I put Oscar back in his cage and put some food in his dish. I sat back for a moment to watch him munch. It felt good to be with Oscar. When I was with him, I could be myself and not worry about anything else. Oscar's life was simple.

Sniff. Eat. Hide. Explore. Poop. Sleep.

There was a tap on my bedroom door.

"Where did you and Ryan disappear to tonight?" Mom asked, stepping into the room. "I was going to ask you to play your minuet for everyone."

"That's what I was afraid of," I muttered.

"What do you mean, Conner?" Mom demanded.

"You know I don't like playing in front of people."

"But you've got a recital coming up. You have to get used to playing in front of an audience," Mom insisted.

"Why? What's the point?"

"Conner," Mom said sharply. "We've been through this before."

She sighed and sat down on my bed, gesturing for me to sit beside her. "Playing the piano takes dedication and hard work," she continued in a patient voice. "It may not seem like much fun right now, but later you'll thank your dad and me for making you stick with it."

I opened my mouth to object.

"I wish I'd had the opportunity to learn to play the piano when I was your age," Mom went on.

Frustration bubbled up inside me.

"But that's you, Mom. Not me," I said. "Maybe *you* should take piano lessons."

Mom looked at me in surprise, then laughed.

"I'm serious," I said.

She smiled and shook her head.

"I wouldn't want to inflict that on the rest of you," she said dismissively. "I don't have time, anyway."

She got up off the bed, ready to leave, then caught sight of Oscar's cage.

"You should wash your hands after you've been touching that rat," she said.

I rolled my eyes, the frustration building pressure in my chest. She hadn't listened to anything I'd said.

"Mom," I called after her. What could I say to make her understand?

She paused in the doorway, and I took a deep breath.

"You know how you like cooking?" I began.

"Yes," she answered slowly, not sure what I was getting at.

"It's something you love, and you're good at it," I continued. "But Ma Ma doesn't seem to notice."

"Conner!" Mom exclaimed, taken aback. I pressed on.

"Well, that's how *I* feel too," I said. "No one notices or cares what *I* like and what *I'm* good at."

Mom's expression softened.

"Oh, Conner," she said, reaching out to me. I pulled away, and Mom winced. She took a breath.

"If you're worried about the recital," she continued, "we don't expect you to play as well as Jenna."

I almost screamed.

"That's my whole point, Mom," I said. "You *do* expect me to be as good as Jenna. But I'm *not* Jenna. I'm me. Jenna loves piano. I hate it!"

I pushed past her and stomped out of the room, flinging more words as I went.

"You don't even know *what* I like. You don't know anything about me!"

"Conner, wait. Where are you going?" Mom called after me.

"I'm going to wash my hands!" I answered, not looking back.

The next day was piano lesson day. I got up and got ready, as usual, but I felt like there was a huge weight pressing down on me. I'd tried to tell Mom how I felt, but nothing had changed.

When I entered the kitchen, Mom was making coffee. She turned to me as if she wanted to say something, but then Jenna followed me into the room.

"Morning, Mom," Jenna said, ignoring me. "Can we make pancakes?"

"What do you think, Conner?" Mom asked. "Would you like pancakes?"

"I'll just have cereal," I said in a dull voice.

For a second Mom looked hurt, but I didn't care. She couldn't just fix everything with food.

"Well, I want some!" Jenna piped up, not noticing what was going on between Mom and me. "And I bet Dad does too."

Mom dug out the frying pan, and Jenna got the eggs and milk from the fridge. I turned my back on them and determinedly carried my bowl and cereal to the table.

Soon the delicious aroma of pancakes filled the room. I stuffed a spoonful of cereal into my mouth and tried to ignore the smell.

"Hey, something smells good," Dad said as he strode into the kitchen, hair damp, face freshly shaved. "What's the occasion?"

"Since when do I need a special occasion to cook for my family?" Mom joked. "Besides, it's New Year's Eve tonight."

"Does that mean you're making Chinese pancakes?" Dad teased.

"No, we're making *my* pancakes," Mom said, giving me a quick pointed look. Was she trying to tell me something?

I shoveled in the last of my cereal and pushed my chair away from the table.

"I better get going," I said to nobody in particular.

I rode my bike to Miss Remple's house. The roads were wet from the rain that had fallen in the night. I parked my bike outside the studio at the back of Miss Remple's house and knocked on the door. Miss Remple answered, coffee cup in hand.

"Come in, Conner," she said with her usual smile.

I stepped into the warmth of the studio and into the sickly sweet odor of her coffee and perfume, the familiar queasy feeling waking in me. The smell seemed worse than usual today. I hung up my coat on the rack by the door and took a deep calming breath while my back was to Miss Remple. Come on, I told myself. What's one more piano lesson? Then, imagining a prisoner pulling together his courage before facing a firing squad, I squared my shoulders, turned and walked over to the piano bench.

I propped my music book up on the piano and readied my fingers over the keys.

"Let's warm up with some scales," Miss Remple said as if she were going to join in, which, of course, she wasn't.

As she took her place behind me, there was a waft of perfume and coffee and the sound of a sip. I braced myself for the swallowing gurgle and plunked my fingers onto the keys, beginning the first scale

"All right," Miss Remple said when I'd finished. "Let's see how the minuet is coming."

I took another deep breath, trying to loosen the heaviness that dragged at me. I fumbled through the pages of my music book, readied my fingers over the keys and began.

Before I was halfway through, there was an unexpected touch on my shoulder. I jumped, then winced at the jarring sound that rose out of the piano as my fingers hit the wrong keys.

"Sorry, Conner," Miss Remple said quietly. "I didn't mean to startle you. Stop there for a minute, please."

She didn't have to tell me twice to stop. I waited, relieved at the reprieve, but puzzled. Miss Remple stood up and set her coffee cup down on top of the piano. She looked down at me silently for a moment, and I began to feel uncomfortable. Maybe she really was going to interrogate me this time.

But instead she sighed and smiled sadly.

"Your heart isn't in this, is it?" she said. She didn't seem angry. "Is there something you want to tell me?"

I sat there for a second, stunned. Then it was like a door had opened in front of me, and I went through it.

"I don't want to play the piano," I blurted.

I expected her to get mad or start in on the importance of practicing and how playing well doesn't always come easily. But she didn't.

"Have you talked to your parents about this?" she asked. If anything, she sounded sympathetic.

"I've tried," I said. "But they won't listen. I'm sorry, Miss Remple. I think you're a good teacher and all, and piano music can sound really nice when someone like you or Jenna plays it. But…" I trailed off.

"It doesn't matter how well you can play," Miss Remple said carefully. "What matters is how you feel about it.It should be something you love and enjoy—not a chore that you hate."

I looked down, reddening slightly.

"Hmm," Miss Remple said. "So it's that way, is it?"

She touched my shoulder again.

"You don't have to apologize to me if your passion is somewhere else," she said, "but I think you need to tell your parents."

Easier said than done. I turned to her.

"Could you talk to them?" I asked. "Please? They might listen to you."

Miss Remple sighed and looked tired.

"I'll give your parents a call," she said, "but you have to promise to talk to them as well. Okay?"

Relief swept through me.

"Okay," I told her.

"Now," she reached for her coffee mug, "I don't think there's any point in continuing the lesson today, do you?"

"I guess not," I said, trying not to sound as thrilled as I felt.

"So I'll get myself some more coffee and make that phone call," she said. "And you can head home."

My elation nosedived.

Mom and Dad were not going to be happy about this.

I scooped up my music books, and Miss Remple followed me to the door.

"Don't forget your coat," she said.

"Oh, right."

She opened the door for me as I slipped on my jacket. I felt like I was outside my body, watching myself move. This was so unreal. Had I just quit piano lessons?

"Bye, Miss Remple," I said awkwardly. "Thanks."

"Good luck," she said, giving me a wave and an encouraging smile.

I'll need it, I thought as I climbed on my bike. What were Mom and Dad going to say?

Complication

The air was cold and the pavement damp as I headed for home. I pedaled in a daze, not thinking about where I was going. How were Mom and Dad going to react to Miss Remple's call? Would they let me quit piano? Would they be very disappointed? Would they ground me more? What about practicing for the bike competition? What about Oscar? My thoughts roiled like a dark storm cloud.

Suddenly a car door opened in front of me. In a flash I realized I was going to hit it. In that same instant I slammed on the brakes and jerked the bike sideways. There was a bone-jarring thud and a wave of pain. Then blackness.

I woke up in the hospital with Mom and Dad standing over me. I was lying on a stretcher. Pain pulsed through my body. What was going on?

"Oh, Conner," Mom whispered, noticing my eyes open. She had tears in hers.

"How do you feel, son?" Dad asked, leaning closer.

"Sore," I groaned, not quite able to identify which parts hurt and which parts didn't. "How long have I been here?"

"It's been about half an hour since your accident," Mom said.

"My accident?" I asked groggily, noticing that my head was one of the things that hurt—though not as much as my right shoulder and thigh.

"Someone in a parked car opened their door right in front of you," Dad explained, sounding angry, but not at me. "The doctor says you managed to hit sideways somehow instead of hitting straight on and flying over the handlebars."

"That's right," the doctor said as she stepped up to the stretcher. "In these types of accidents, cyclists tend to suffer head and upper body trauma, but you seem to have gotten off better than most."

Dad reached out to rest a hand on my head.

"He's good at bike maneuvers," Dad said proudly.

My eyes darted to Dad in surprise.

"So nothing's broken?" I asked, turning my gaze back to the doctor.

"Nope," the doctor said. "Just some nasty bruises."

She leaned over me and shone a flashlight into my eyes.

"But you did hit your head on the pavement when you fell after the impact with the door," she pointed out. "And you have a bit of a concussion."

"I thought I didn't hit my head."

"Not initially and not at high speed," the doctor explained. "Plus, you were wearing a helmet. But we do need to keep an eye on you for a bit."

"Are you sure he's okay?" Mom asked, her voice anxious.

"He'll be fine," the doctor said.

"There's no internal damage?" Dad asked.

"It doesn't look that way," the doctor answered. "But I'd like to do some tests to be on the safe side."

"What happened to my bike?" I asked, trying to sit up, which I immediately regretted. Pain and blackness washed over me.

"You better not try getting up quite yet," the doctor said, noting the look on my face.

Mom and Dad pressed closer.

"Don't worry about your bike," Dad said. "It's okay."

I wanted to ask how much damage there was to the bike, but I was suddenly very tired. The room was getting blurry. I closed my eyes.

When I opened my eyes again, the doctor was gone. I was in a different room and lying on a proper bed—at least a proper bed for a hospital. The room was dim, and Mom was sitting in a chair by the window.

"Mom?"

She jumped up and came to stand by my bed.

"How are you feeling?" she asked softly, reaching out to touch my face.

"Better." My whole body no longer felt like one big bruise. The soreness now seemed to be concentrated in my shoulder and thigh, and my head no longer hurt.

"That's good," Mom said with a smile. "The doctor gave you a shot of pain medication. It must be working."

"Where's Dad?"

"He's gone downstairs to get some coffee," Mom said. "He'll be right back."

Coffee. My stomach did a flip-flop as I suddenly remembered the smell of Miss Remple's coffee and perfume. The piano lesson! It all came back to me then. Had Miss Remple called Mom and Dad? Were they mad? Would they let me quit piano?

"Miss Remple—" I began, struggling to sit up.

"Shh," Mom said, easing me back down. "Miss Remple called us about your piano lessons. We'll talk about it later. I don't want you to worry about anything right now."

Her voice was soft and comforting. Not mad at all. I lay back down and closed my eyes again.

"Just rest now," Mom's voice continued. "Think of being in the hospital as being on a holiday."

A holiday? My eyes popped open, and I tried to get up again.

"How long am I going to be in here?" I demanded.

"Just until they've done some tests," Mom said. "Maybe overnight."

"I can't stay overnight! I have to get home and feed Oscar."

Gently, Mom pushed me back down again.

"I said I didn't want you to worry about anything," Mom said firmly, but with a smile. "Your Dad and I will go home and check on Oscar."

"But you don't know what to feed him."

"We'll figure it out. He'll be fine."

Her hand rested on my chest, its weight comforting. I closed my eyes once more and this time drifted into sleep. At the edge of my consciousness, the worries hovered like the shadows in the corners of the room.

Release

By the next morning I was feeling foolish about being stuck in the hospital with nothing but a slight headache and bruises. My whole body felt kind of stiff when I got up to use the bathroom, but at least I could do that now. I wondered if I'd still be sore for the bike competition— or if I'd even have a bike to ride.

I pressed the controls on the side of my bed to raise myself to a sitting position and pointed the TV remote at the small television fixed to the wall in front of my bed. My parents must have dished out some extra money to get me this private room with a TV. When I pressed the *On* button, voices filled the room, but they weren't just coming from the TV.

I turned to see Erika and Mercedes walk through the door, followed by Jake, who hung back a bit, looking embarrassed.

"Hey," Jake said, pushing forward. "Pretty extreme way to get out of piano lessons."

Everyone laughed, which eased the awkwardness, though the comment felt a little too close for comfort to me. I flicked off the TV.

"How did you guys know I was here?" I asked.

"I called your house," Jake answered. "Your sister told me what happened."

"Then he called me," Erika added.

I looked at Jake with surprise but didn't say anything.

"So what did you break?" Jake asked.

"Nothing," I said.

"You're really lucky," Mercedes said. "My cousin ran into a parked car once. Broke his nose, and his whole face had to be bandaged up."

"I didn't *run* into the car," I pointed out. "The driver opened his door into me."

"Who's taking care of Oscar?" Erika asked.

"My mom and dad, I guess."

Jake raised an eyebrow.

"Or maybe they asked Jenna to do it," I said.

"Maybe they took him back to the shelter," Jake suggested.

Mercedes jabbed him in the ribs with her elbow.

"Don't say that," she told him. "Of course they didn't take Oscar back to the shelter."

A nurse walked in with a stethoscope around her neck and a blood pressure cuff in her hand. My friends stepped back while the nurse wrapped the cuff around my upper left arm and began pumping air into it.

"You're welcome to stay," she said to them, but they were backing toward the door.

"We've got to go anyway," Mercedes said.

"Hope we see you at school tomorrow," Erika added.

"Yeah," Jake said as he ducked through the door. "Have fun."

I would have thrown my pillow after him, but I didn't think the nurse would be too happy if I did. So I sat back quietly and let her finish checking me over. My mind went back to Jake's earlier words. Could Mom and Dad really have taken Oscar back to the shelter? My insides twisted with frustration—like a tied-up prisoner. I needed to get home to check on Oscar.

Finally, around noon, Dad showed up to take me home. We sat in the car in silence for the first couple of blocks. Then I took a deep breath.

"Dad," I began, "I'm really sorry about piano. I did try my hardest. Honest."

Dad was quiet for a moment, and I held my breath, my hands turning sweaty.

"I know you did," he said at last, and I let out my breath with relief.

"Maybe we were pushing you too hard," Dad continued. "Maybe you just need a break from piano for a while."

I didn't think a break was all I needed, but it was a start, and I didn't complain.

"Listen," he said, glancing over at me. "I've seen you work hard at things—taking care of that rat and practicing your bike tricks. I'm a bit disappointed with how the piano worked out…but, Conner, I'm not disappointed in you. No way."

Keeping one hand on the steering wheel, Dad reached out his other hand to give the top of my head a quick rub.

I leaned back in my seat, a warm feeling in my chest. I realized, as we drove the rest of the way home, that even if I didn't get to keep Oscar, I was pretty lucky.

On the drive home, Dad assured me that Oscar was okay and that no one had returned him to the shelter behind my back. All the same, I felt apprehensive as I entered the house and headed to my room. Mom had been alone with Oscar all morning. What if he'd gotten out of his cage and she'd panicked and hit him with the broom or something?

No, that was a stupid thought. She wouldn't do anything like that. But as I took the last steps to my bedroom, I couldn't help feeling something was wrong. Why was the house so quiet? Dad was outside doing something in the yard, but where was Mom? The door to Jenna's bedroom was closed, and I could hear her voice inside, probably talking on the phone to one of her friends. That, at least, was normal. But my own door was partway open. I never left it like that. I kept it either open or closed, not in-between. As I stepped up to the door, part of the room was blocked from my view, but through the gap I could see Oscar's cage sitting on the floor. I froze.

The door on the top of the cage hung open. The cage was empty.

Sharing Oscar

I rushed into the room, then stopped short. Mom was kneeling on the floor by the bed, looking down at something on the bed that was sitting on top of a towel. It was Oscar. He was peeking out from a cardboard tube, sniffing the air. Mom looked up, startled.

"Conner! I didn't hear you come in."

She got to her feet and gave me a hug, careful not to squeeze my sore side.

"Are you feeling all right?" Mom asked. "Do you need to sit down?"

"I'm okay," I assured her, but I sat down on the end of the bed anyway and held out my hand to Oscar.

As if he recognized me (or perhaps my voice), Oscar took a few steps out of the tube, eager to sniff my fingers.

"I think he missed you," said Mom.

I looked up at her, feeling like something was wrong with this picture.

"I thought you didn't like Oscar," I said.

Mom gave me an embarrassed smile.

"I guess he's not so bad once you get used to him," she said.

I grinned. "You actually picked him up?"

Mom smiled back.

"I did indeed," she said, looking proud of herself. "You said he needed exercise, didn't you?"

I nodded.

"Although he hasn't had much," she commented. "Except for his dash to the tube."

"He feels safer in there," I pointed out. "Rats don't like open spaces."

"Oh," Mom said. "I guess that makes sense."

"What did you feed him?" I asked.

"That stuff you had in that bag by the cage?"

"All of it?" I asked incredulously. There had been enough food there to last at least a couple of days.

"Wasn't I supposed to?" Mom asked. "He kept emptying out his dish, so I thought he needed more."

I laughed. "Let me show you something," I said.

Carefully, I knelt down on the floor beside Oscar's cage, my sore shoulder and leg protesting. I started to reach into the cage with my right arm, felt a twinge of pain and switched to my left arm. I grabbed Oscar's house and lifted it up. Under the house was a pile of food.

"Oh," Mom said.

"He likes to horde things," I explained. "If I let him loose in the house, he'd collect other stuff, as well."

"Hmm," Mom said. "But you won't be doing that, will you?"

"No," I said quickly, regretting my choice of words.

Mom seemed to regret hers as well. She sighed and bent down to help me up.

"I know you're doing a good job with the rat," she said.

"You mean *Oscar*," I said.

"With Oscar," she continued, smiling slightly. "But you're going to have to take it easy this week, you know."

"I'm fine," I protested, growing alarmed. "I can take care of him." Was she going to suggest we return him to the shelter early?

"I know, I know," Mom said, holding up her hands. "I'm just saying I want you to take it easy and let Jenna and Dad and me help you with things."

"Okay," I said, relieved. "I will."

"Now, do you want me to put Oscar back in the cage for you?" she asked. "I want you to rest."

"I can do it," I told her. "I'm just going to lie on the bed with him for a while."

Mom frowned and opened her mouth as if she was going to protest. She probably wanted to warn me about rat germs. But then she looked over at Oscar, who was sitting at the opening to his tunnel, licking his paws and wiping them over his face—as if to show her how clean he was.

Mom sighed.

"All right," she said hesitantly. "But try to keep him on the old towel I put out. I don't want him peeing on your bed."

I rolled my eyes. Same old Mom.

I climbed onto the bed and stretched out on my left side beside Oscar. Mom started to leave but paused in the doorway and looked back.

"I do know about some of the things you like," she said softly and with a nod at Oscar. "I'm sorry if it seems like I haven't been paying attention."

I looked at Mom with surprise. She *had* heard what I'd been trying to tell her the other night. She appeared to be trying not to cry.

"It's okay, Mom," I said quickly, giving her a smile.

She leaned against the doorframe.

"And I know you like those bike tricks too," she went on. "Your dad says you're good at them."

I couldn't help grinning.

"Dad said that?"

"Yes." She smiled. "He also said you've got some kind of competition coming up."

I nodded, but my face fell as I remembered my bike.

"If I've got a bike to ride," I said glumly.

"Don't worry about your bike," she said. "Your dad

already took it to the bike shop to be fixed. Just worry about taking care of yourself."

She waited for me to nod, then smiled again.

"Okay then," she said.

The next moment, Oscar and I were alone. I looked down and held out a finger for him to sniff. Maybe things weren't so bad after all. The thought was bittersweet. In five days I'd have to take Oscar back to the shelter.

Last Days

On Monday I was still pretty stiff and sore, so Mom gave me a ride to school. After school, Jenna helped me clean Oscar's cage.

"I hope you don't have to do this every day," she grumbled.

"I scoop the poop out every day," I explained, "but I only change the bedding every couple of days."

She groaned.

"Well, you better feel better soon," she complained, but when we were finished cleaning, she smiled and offered Oscar a piece of cereal.

"I think he needs more variety in his diet," she said to me. Then to Oscar she added, "Don't you, little guy?" in the kind of high-pitched cutesy voice girls use to talk to babies or stuffed animals. I rolled my eyes.

"He'll eat anything," I said with a shrug. "But I don't think he got any fruit or vegetables while I was away."

"I better get you something then," she told Oscar in the same dumb voice.

Jenna jumped up and headed to the kitchen. I shook my head, watching her scurry off. She was still annoying, but somehow she no longer seemed so bad.

In a couple of minutes, Jenna was back, followed by Mom. Their arms were piled with food.

"What do you think he'd like?" Mom asked, holding out an apple and a plastic container of leftover pasta.

I laughed.

"Well, a tiny piece of everything, I guess."

That night, Dad checked in on me when I had Oscar out on my bed. "How are you doing?" he asked.

"Pretty good," I told him.

He glanced at Oscar, who was peeking out of his hiding spot under a fold in my duvet cover. Oscar twitched his nose at Dad.

"Inquisitive little guy," Dad commented.

"Yeah. Curious, but cautious," I said.

"Hmm," Dad said as he turned to go.

I wondered what he was thinking, but it was hard to tell. He didn't seem to dislike Oscar, but I wasn't sure he liked him either. Only a few more days left until I had to take Oscar back to the shelter. Was there any chance Mom and Dad would change their minds by then?

The rest of the week went by too quickly. On Wednesday, at the animal club meeting, Erika said she'd heard that the SPCA now had custody of the animals they'd seized from the pet store. That meant that the animals we'd been looking after were now available for adoption.

The girls thought this was good news.

"Now Missy and the others can get real homes," Mercedes said.

But all I could think about was losing Oscar. Friday after school I'd have to give him up.

"There's no guarantee they're all going to find homes," Erika pointed out. "What if no one wants them?"

"We can help find homes for them," Annie suggested.

"Good idea," Mercedes said. "We can put up posters around the school and at the community center and the grocery stores." Her voice began to rise with excitement.

"We still have some time today," Erika said. "We could start working on the posters now."

"I'm no good at drawing stuff," Jake interjected, looking over from where he stood by Daisy's habitat.

"You can't be any worse than me," Sean told him. "You don't have to be Rembrandt to get the message across."

"What do you think, Conner?" Erika asked. "You haven't said anything yet."

I shrugged.

"I guess I don't want anyone to adopt Oscar," I admitted. "Unless it's me."

By Thursday afternoon I was feeling sick at the thought of having to give up Oscar. Jenna was already practicing the piano when I got home from school, and I was only slightly cheered by the thought that I didn't have to practice anymore.

At suppertime I sat at the table, poking at the food on my plate with my fork.

"Conner, why aren't you eating?" Mom asked. "You don't feel sick, do you?"

"No," I said, shrugging. "I guess I'm just not hungry."

Mom and Dad gave each other a look across the table.

Jenna, who sat opposite me, looked up and mouthed the word *Oscar*, with a questioning look on her face.

I shrugged again, but Jenna knew she'd got it right.

After supper I went straight to my room. No one objected.

"Hey, Oscar," I called out, kneeling down beside his cage on the floor.

At the sound of my voice, Oscar scrambled up to the roof of his little house and stretched out his twitching nose to greet me. I let him smell my fingers for a moment; then I opened the door to his cage and lifted him out.

I held him in my hands, savoring the feel of his soft warm body. His tiny heart beat against my skin through his fur. I lifted him up to my face and looked him in the eyes. Our noses touched.

What was he thinking in his little rat head? Did he sense anything different about tonight? Would he mind being back at the shelter? Would he even notice it wasn't me coming to feed him anymore?

I sighed and set Oscar down on top of my bed. I hoped he'd be adopted quickly at least, and that his new family would be kind to him and let him out of his cage for exercise.

Oscar stood for a moment in the middle of the bed, sniffing the air. He wasn't as afraid as he had been when I'd brought him home two weeks ago. I wrinkled up the duvet cover to make him a tunnel, and he ducked into it. I'd made a long, twisting wrinkle, and I placed a Cheerio at the far end, wondering how long it would take him to discover it there.

I sat down on the bed, carefully, just as Oscar's pink nose popped out of the opposite end of the tunnel. He snatched up the Cheerio and disappeared again. I couldn't help laughing. That was the great thing about Oscar: He always made me laugh. Just looking at his kinked whiskers was enough to make me smile.

It was hard to put Oscar back in his cage that night. I put it off as long as I could. I left him on my bed when I went to brush my teeth, closing my bedroom door so that he couldn't get out of the room if he decided to climb off the bed. When I got back to my room, Oscar was sitting on my pillow, as if he too was ready for bed.

"Sorry, Oscar," I said, picking him up. "I don't think Mom would be too happy if I let you sleep with me."

I placed Oscar back in his cage, added a few treats to his food dish, checked his water, then reluctantly closed the cage door. When I stood up again, my eyes were caught by the thick book lying on my desk. I hadn't picked up *The Complete Guide to Dogs* since I'd gotten Oscar. I hadn't even thought about wanting a dog for two weeks. After Oscar went back to the shelter tomorrow, things would go back to how they had been before. No pets.

Maybe some things had changed. It felt like Mom and Dad were finally seeing *me*—not just who they wanted me to be. That felt good, but at the moment it did little to raise my spirits. By tomorrow night, Oscar would be gone.

Return to the Shelter

I got Oscar's cage and supplies all ready to go in the morning before school. After school, Mom would pack them into the car, pick me up from school and drive us to the shelter.

All day at school it was hard to concentrate. Erika and Mercedes kept flashing me looks of sympathy, which made things worse. Other people caught on and wondered what was up.

Once Jake elbowed me in the ribs and teased, "Your girlfriends are looking at you."

"Shut up! " I told him a little more loudly than I'd meant to. Miss Chien gave me a warning look, and I slumped down in my seat.

It was the kind of day I'd normally wish would end quickly. But today the end meant giving up Oscar. It wasn't the same for Erika and the others. When Erika brought her rats back to the shelter, she would still have three dogs at home. Mercedes said she'd miss her foster hamster, but she was looking forward to getting a good night's sleep. Annie claimed she would not miss her rabbit at all, since he didn't seem to like her anyway, and it would be a lot safer for the rabbit back at the shelter. He'd chewed through so many electrical cords at her house, her parents were more than ready to be rid of him.

When the bell rang to signal the end of the school day, it jangled through my body. Slowly I packed my homework into my backpack and dragged my feet out of the classroom. Mom was waiting for me with the car in front of the school.

I climbed into the passenger seat, mumbling a greeting. Craning my head, I saw that Oscar's cage sat on a towel on the seat behind me. I faced forward again and sat stiffly as the car pulled away from the school.

After a couple of blocks of silence, Mom glanced over at me and frowned.

"You really don't want to give him up, do you?" she asked.

I shook my head, though I thought the answer was pretty obvious.

"I was afraid this would happen," Mom went on. "Your dad and I talked last night—about the possibility of keeping him."

My heart leapt and I spun to face her. But she was shaking her head, her forehead still furrowed.

"I don't know," she continued. "We do agree that Oscar's not a lot of trouble, and you've been taking good care of him…There's the extra garbage from his cage, which I don't like—"

"But I put it out before you even see it," I said, quickly.

"I know. But there are times when we'll be away on holiday."

"One of my friends could look after him then," I pressed, not sure if I should dare to hope.

She continued to frown.

"I'm still not happy with the way you went behind our backs," she said. "And I don't like rewarding bad behavior."

I looked down.

"I know," I said. "I shouldn't have brought him home without your permission, and I shouldn't have let the shelter think I had it."

But was I sorry? I felt bad about disappointing Mom and Dad and about breaking their trust. But I was glad that I'd had Oscar—even just for two weeks.

Mom turned the car into the shelter parking lot and pulled into a vacant spot. Slowly I climbed out of the car and opened the back door. Oscar stood up to greet me.

"Hang on, Oscar," I whispered as I picked up the cage.

He scurried into the safety of his house.

Mom opened the door to the shelter, and I maneuvered through it, then carried the cage up to the front desk.

"What can I do for you today?" a young man greeted us.

"Umm…I've been fostering this rat," I made myself explain.

"Oh, that's right," the man interjected. "Mini told me to expect you kids."

He looked at Mom. "So you're bringing this one back, are you?"

I swallowed.

"Yeah," I began. But Mom put her hand on mine, halting my words.

She took a deep breath.

"No," she said. "We'd like to adopt him."

My mouth dropped open, and I think I might even have gasped. The man looked us both over and grinned.

"All right, then," he said. "I'll get the contract."

As soon as he turned away, I twisted around to look into Mom's face.

"For real?" I asked.

Mom sighed again and smiled, nodding her head.

"At least he doesn't bark," she said.

I laughed. I'd forgotten how loud the barking of the dogs in the kennels sounded when you first visited the shelter. Right then it was like a muffled off-key chorus.

The man returned to the counter with a sheet of paper.

"Well," he began, "I assume you already know how to provide a good home for the rat, since you've been taking care of him for…what has it been?"

"Two weeks," I said.

"And you've got permission from your landlord, if you're renting?"

"We have our own house," I said. "And yes, I've got permission." I nodded toward Mom, and the man smiled.

I have it this time, I thought, still feeling amazed that my mom had changed her mind.

Mom leaned over to sign the contract, agreeing that we'd take proper care of Oscar.

"He's all yours," the man said.

I took a firm grip on Oscar's cage again and lifted it off the counter. Mom laughed when she saw my face. I guess I was smiling pretty much from ear to ear. As we turned to leave, Erika's dad walked through the door and held it open for Erika and Mercedes, who held cages in their arms.

"Aren't you headed the wrong way?" Erika's dad asked after saying hello.

"No," I said, still grinning.

Erika and Mercedes looked from my face to my mom's and then back to the piece of paper in Mom's hand.

"You're adopting him?" Erika asked, her eyes wide.

"Apparently," Mom answered, as if she didn't quite believe it herself.

I nodded, trying to get my goofy grin under control. But then Mercedes squealed and attempted to hug me, knocking her hamster's cage against Oscar's. I could feel my face turning red. Everyone laughed, but I didn't mind.

Erika's dad was still holding the shelter door open, so we said goodbye and headed through it. As I walked to the car with Oscar close to my chest, my whole body felt light and free.

"We're going home, Oscar," I whispered.

While doing research for this book, **Jacqueline Pearce** fostered a rat named Oscar from an SPCA shelter. Jacqueline is the author of *Dog House Blues*, *Discovering Emily*, *Emily's Dream* and *The Reunion*, all published by Orca. She lives in Burnaby, British Columbia, where she and her cat are responsible for keeping uninvited rats out of the house.